Urban Excel

Laced Panties

...AN EROTIC DRAMA

By
Imonie Sincere

© 2019 Imonie Sincere

All rights reserved. No part of this book may be used or reproduced, distributed, or transmitted in any manner, including but not limited to, photocopying, recording, or other electronic or mechanical methods, without written permission from the author, except in the case of brief quotations embodied in critical articles or reviews.

Laced Panties – An Erotic Drama

Presented by: Urban Excellence Entertaiment
Urbanexcellenceent.com

ISBN: 9798688859102

Printed in the United States
10 9 8 7 6 5 4 3 2

For more information or to contact the author, please go to:

@imoniesincere on Instagram.com

Acknowledgements

All praises to The Most High God for allowing me another opportunity to entertain the world through the vivid lens of creative excellence in the form of a pen and pad while allowing me to remain humble in the process. To my son Ivan Ross daddy loves you and will forever be proud of you. To the Queen of my universe —you know who are; thank you for constantly giving the encouragement needed even though I know I can get on your last nerves lol… Love you though beautiful! Bless up Mom as you already know you're my favorite woman in the whole world—we got another classic novel to set the streets on fire! Much love Pops as I'm forever proud of the great man that you are, my siblings Feirious(Fee) you'll be home soon greater than ever, Federed Jr.(@_ykingJunior), Tykia, Tigeria and all my nieces and nephews(To many to name all!). Much love Uncle Pat, Uncle L, Uncle Calvin, Uncle Skeet, Drae, Lil Calvin, Aunt Tammy, Aunt Kakie, Aunt Renee, Aunt Rab, Aunt Becky, Shyeeda, Stacy, Uncle Bookie, Uncle Kenny, Federed Sr. and any other relatives not mentioned just know I love y'all too. To my brother from another mother; Kenny Sparks(@original_hotboy6), thank you for always keeping it 100 having my back when times were tough. To my friends that been down from day one: Saw-Money, Shak, J-Black, Syke, Champ, White Boy Doug, Big Bruh Snapkatt, Cook, J-Baby, Trip, JimmyMac, Official Chyna, BigHeadBob, Dwan Red, Renata Hannans The Hope Dealer and so many more of y'all that know it's all love when I see you. To any and all who've been supporting my work much love from the core of my being. To the beautiful ladies that unknowingly offer inspiration for my lovely and exciting characters I thank you with your sexy self. The radio stations that allowed me to interview and promote my work: NextUpTv, StrongArm Radio, MatureLife Radio, Battle of the Barnes Podcast and many more thank you so much for the opportunities. To my brothers and sisters standing tall behind those gates of oppression keep fighting and shining as you're needed out here in society and will be forever missed until your return. With that said let the journey of sexual sensuality begin as the soft panties will fall where they may and mentally arouse you to your highest pinnacles of ecstasy and moistened drama! Peace and blessings Kings and Queens from your favorite author Imonie Sincere....

A woman never quite feels desired and appreciated enough. She wants attention, but a man is often distracted and unresponsive. The Rake is a great female fantasy figure—when he desires a woman, brief though that moment may be, he will go to the ends of the earth for her. He may be disloyal, dishonest, and amoral, but that only adds to his appeal. Unlike the normal, cautious male, the Rake is delightfully unrestrained, a slave to his love of women. There is the added lure of his reputation: so many women have succumbed to him, there has to be a reason. Words are a woman's weakness, and the Rake is a master of seductive language. Stir a woman's repressed longings by adapting the Rake's mix of danger and pleasure.

~~~ Art of Seduction by Robert Greene

Prologue

"Girl I know I'll get my man to put it down good all night if I come in the bedroom with this on!" Deja remarked holding up a light blue lingerie set.

"If you go in wearing nothing you'll probably get the same affect,", Unique chimed in with a high five. Unique and Deja were panty shopping inside the newly-established JUICY DRIPZ© casual night wear store inside the Pines Mall in Broward County, Florida. There wasn't a special occasion but these two women just like all women loved the feeling of putting on a new pair of sexy panties.

"Girl you a trip," Deja replied laughing.

"Nawl girl I'mma tell you who a trip."

"Who?" Deja questioned thinking that Unique had some gossip hot off the press.

"Don't look but dude over there wit his ole lady keep watching us," Unique mentioned.

"You wanna get him in trouble?" Deja inquired sinisterly.

"How?"

"Juss follow my lead." Deja began grabbing different

garments sizing them up to her body posing seductively occasionally staring into the guy's lustful eyes. Unique joined in on the fun also. He literally forgot he was in the store with his lady until she slapped him very hard in the back of his neck awaking him from his lustful aroused daze.

"What you doing?" he questioned wiping the drool attempting to fall from his lips.

"No, what you doin! You eye-fucking these women up in here right in front of me. Ooh I knew you wasn't no good!" the girlfriend ranted as an argument was fueled by her insecurities and his blatant disrespect. No longer wanting to shop the girl stormed out the store with the guy behind attempting to explain. Deja and Unique erupted in laughter enjoying the live entertainment.

"Girl you still ain't lost a step," Unique praised attempting to quell her laughter.

"And you haven't either wit yo badd self."

"Shut yo mouth," Unique commented continuing to chuckle.

Chapter 1

"Girl so you telling me it was good like that?!"

"Good ain't the word. Gurl the dude was hung like he came directly from the Mandingo tribe itself," Lacy replied giggling nearly having an orgasm at the thought. Lacy Hankerson embodied the L-7 type goody two-shoes; or at least that's the image she always maintained in public. Lacy stood five foot nine slightly bowlegged with a coke bottle physique. Her almond brown eyes complemented a caramel bronzed complexion, topped off with ebony colored hair that rested just below the shoulders.

"Well high-five to you then!" Monica exclaimed femininly slapping palms with her. Monica Pryce was the owner of a international travel agency that was renowned for their exquisite services. She was equal to Lacy in height, with caramel color eyes and a peanut butter skin tone. Monica donned neatly twisted dreadlocks with blonde tips that would hang down to the middle of her back if she ever let them loose from the uniquely styled bun pinned up.

"Yes girrl! I might call him again tonight the way this Long

Island Iced Tea got me feeling," Lacy admitted sipping the last of her liquor through a neon colored straw. The two ladies were hanging out at Blue Martini for Tuesday evening Happy Hour, allowing the relaxing ambiance of Fort Lauderdale Beach to ease their pent-up after a long day of working.

"Don't stop get it get it!" Monica exclaimed slightly twerking on the barstool imitating a 90s classic tune from Uncle Luke and the 2 Live Crew.

"Girl you a mess," Lacy responded laughing lightheartedly.

"But yeah chic I don't wanna get to tipsy because I need to stay focused on my drive home."

"Yeah me too," Lacy agreed arising from the barstool. They exited the bar to the sounds of a live jazz band playing behind them. Upon sharing goodbyes they agreed to meet up Friday night downtown Las Olas. Behind the tents of the 5 Series BMW Lacy was reminiscent to a horny college girl seeking an ecstatic sexual encounter. On her drive towards her Pompano Beach apartment Lacy would sporadically massage her pussy as the sexual urges were too much to bear. Lacy would occasionally grip the steering wheel with two hands as a means to fight off the burning desires, as well to prevent from wrecking out. Upon making it inside her apartment that was decked out with plush furniture Lacy hurried to strip off all articles of clothing heading for a hot shower in hopes the steamy water would negate the sexual pleasure she adamantly desired. When the effects of the warm water wore off Lacy couldn't withstand it any longer as she repeatedly dialed the same number to no avail leaving at least four messages. The guy of interest stimulated Lacy in ways she couldn't fathom in which her raging sexual libido was turned on to the point of no return. As a secondary measure Lacy turned on a porno and began to utilize the vibrating dildo as a means of getting off. Lacy was yearning for more of the good dick that tantalized her pussy walls just days before. Inwardly Lacy was jealous of the black woman performing on the porno video because she was receiving what Lacy wanted; mind blowing sex! Eventually Lacy dozed off to the ooh's and aah's of the participants on the video nowhere near satisfied but fatigue overwhelmed her entire body.

The Louisiana Fish Fry batter glistened to perfection as the shrimp and fish came out the grease a golden brown hue. Complemented by lobster tails and seasoned steak French fries the aroma within the kitchen was tantalizing. More than willing to flaunt his skills Casanova also known as King to those whom were fond of him, did the honors of cooking. In the meantime Dejanae chilled out watching a reality sitcom on B.E.T.. Dejanae; owner of LAVISH LOOKS BY DEJA was at a point in her life feeling as if the former drama was over and the right man for her had come along. Her shop was continuously thriving in which allowed her to purchase a new vehicle and reclaim her swagger. It had been nearly a year since the abortion of a guy named Taliek's baby which is a phase of life she desired to forget. Life was good and so was Casanova in every aspect especially the category of sex.

"Thanks bae," Deja remarked as Casanova handed her a plate assuring her that men cater to women as well. Deja's island heritage was a major factor in her love for seafood.

"Ain't no pressure. What you want to drink my love?"

"Some of that Minute Maid Berry flavor," Deja responded biting into a shrimp that was dipped in marinara sauce. After preparing a plate for himself Casanova joined Deja on the couch to watch television while they ate.

"Bae I'mma go take a shower to get this seafood smell off me," Casanova remarked after he was done eating.

"I'm coming with you. Lemme' put these dishes in the dishwasher first," Deja replied.

"Alright I'll go warm the water up baby," he mentioned walking into the bedroom. Casanova King or just King for short had the height of six foot one and a half as many would normally say he's six foot two. He had a tree bark brown skin complexion, a perfected 360-degree wave formation on a low brush cut and a chiseled slim built body with a few tattoos inked within his skin. He was nowhere near perfect but Deja loved him plus he reminded her of the man of her former infatuation; Taliek. Casanova was washing himself thoroughly when Deja slid her naked body behind him wrapping her smooth palms around his dick while lightly placing kisses on his back.

"Come on let's clean up so I can take care of you," Casanova remarked as he turned around allowing the water to rinse his soapy flesh.

"Alright give a minute I'll be out daddi." Upon stepping out Casanova brushed his teeth and gargled with minty fresh Listerine, ridding his mouth of any remnants of the seafood dinner. When Deja exited the shower naked reminding Casanova of Keri Hilson he instantly began to rise to attention. Deja noticed the nine and a half inch penis stiffening in which she also became aroused knowing that he knew exactly how to make a woman feel blissfully special with his God -given long stroke. Casanova picked her up as they began kissing passionately. Their sexual organs entertwined without any guidance as Deja slowly began to gyrate her hips. The wetness of her pussy caused his dick to maintain a shimmery gloss as he stroked in and out, side to side also in circular motions. Casanova palmed the cups of her ass cheeks spreading them as he continued to massage deeply inside her tight pussy.

"Yes baby gimme dat dick," Deja moaned in his ear before lightly biting and sucking on his shoulder. Casanova the laid her down on the bed as his hardness remained wedged within her walls placing her legs in the air together constantly jabbing her wetness with long strokes. Eventually he spread her legs in a V-formation allowing her to watch as he worked his hips sliding his moist dick in and out taking her to orgasmic ecstasy.

Never one to cum prematurely Casanova flipped Deja over on her stomach placing a hand in the small of her back as she tooted her ass up slightly----allowing Casanova to get great positioning while beating the pussy up proper.

"Aiigh Casanova, aiigh Casanova, ooh shit daddi! King! Yes King!" Deja purred loudly as multiple orgasms occurred causing her to shiver uncontrollably. Without warning Casanova pulled out and began masturbating. Deja noticed with lustful eyes and began sucking his hard penis until he erupted. His dick seemed to expand an extra inch as semen spewed down Deja's throat.

"Ooh! Daddi you taste like pineapples," Deja remarked swallowing every ounce of his juices.

"I guess that's all dem fruit juices I been drinking."

"Bae you trip," Deja commented laughing. Without forewarning King went down south licking and sucking Deja's pussy as if it was a juicy mango that he been deprived of for years. Deja just lay back in a state of bliss constantly moaning and shaking with each orgasm attained. Deja was in love and every fiber in her body attested to that.

Chapter 2

"Damn this chic blowin me up," Casanova whispered to himself as he pulled his secondary phone out the glove compartment. Cananova had intentions on returning the calls but at the current moment his mind was focused on making money. He wheeled the purple Cadillac Escalade on crome and purple 26-inch rims out the garage headed towards the Oakland Park Flea Market. Casanova opened a small cellphone accessory kiosk booth as he camouflaged his side endeavours. Each day that he opened up for business he intended to make progress towards prosperity no matter how mediocre. As it was rounding noon Casanova received a call on his cellular phone.

"What's up you can't call me back?"

"That's my bad just been kinda busy but what's up?" Casanova responded.

"Uh I was wonderin if I can see you on my lunch break?" Casanova paused contemplating a response then spoke.

"Yeah where you gon be at," he asked knowing exactly what she wanted.

"Meet me at the Miami Subs down the road from my job."

"Aiight I'm on my way now," Casanova responded ending the call. Casanova finished eating the mango salad cup then shutdown the shop momentarily, then rode out towards downtown Fort Lauderdale. When Lacy seen the dark tinted window SUV come to a halt she walked to the passenger door and slid inside.

"What's good cutie?" Casanova inquired with small talk.

"I'm so horny that I haven't been able to function at work."

"Alright climb into the backseat so I can give you a fix," Casanova instructed.

"Thank you. Is two-hundred fifty dollars okay?" Casanova nodded affirming that it was adequate payment for a quickie. As she lay on her back Casanova removed her panties hiking her business skirt up to the waist casually massaging her clit as he stroked his dick to erection in the process.

"Give me that big dick King!" Lacy moaned. King obliged as he rolled a Magnum condom on sliding into her wet pussy. Everything that Lacy craved was being fulfilled at that very opportune moment. Casanova raised up instructing her to turn around, "You gotta go back to work. I can't have ya hair all messed up,". As he stroked her drenched pussy from behind occasionally slapping her ass, Lacy's head would sporadically bump against the door.

"Ooh King fuck me! Yes Kinggg!" Lacy purred in earthly ecstasy. Lacy climaxed three times as Casanova withdrew himself from her wetness pulling the condom off stroking his still erect penis.

"I'll take care of that because I need to eat lunch anyway," Lacy mentioned sucking his long thick dick into a frenzy causing him to cum hard.

"Aargh," he moaned as Lacy swallowed every drop. Temporarily satisfied Lacy straightened out her clothing reaching for her panties.

"I want you to go back without any panties and every time you think about this good dick you gotta play wit ya pussy moaning King ding-a-ling," Casanova ordered staring into her eyes with a sort of mind control. Lacy was into the freaky sex games as well being dickmatized so she willfully obliged while placing her feet back into the grey leather heels. She exited the vehicle after climbing back into the frontseat as if she had a long midday conversation with her lover. Casanova watched intently as her normally tight ass had a loose jiggle as she sashayed back to her vehicle. Inside the 5 series BMW Lacy checked the time realizing her lunch hour concluded in ten minutes. She put on her matching blazer hurriedly driving off into traffic destined for one of the high rise banks downtown where she was a professional financial consultant.

"Aye make sho you tighten up my whip too," Casanova remarked handing over his car keys to NEWPORT SHAWTY. NEWPORT SHAWTY controlled a local car wash operating on the corner of Sunrise Boulevard and 31st avenue intersection at a gas station near the infamous SWAP SHOP. When he went to work cleaning a car it was always done to perfection. The entire time Casanova awaited for his car he conversed on his cellphone portraying the image of the ultimate businessman. NEWPORT SHAWTY directed vehicles into his establishment as if he was an air traffic controller. When he completed cleaning Casanova's ride he was given a fifty-dollar bill.

"Keep the change playa," Casanova commented showing appreciation for the street hustle.

"Alright bet. Aye I ain't know if you wanted to keep dem panties on your backseat so I just left'em where dey was at," NEWPORT SHAWTY mentioned. Casanova paused for a second thinking he was on some sideways freaky shit before responding, "Oh damn I forgot those was back there," laughing simultaneously replaying how they got back there.

"Bet dat up tho," Casanova continued.

"No pressure," NEWPORT SHAWTY replied firing up a cigarette. Within no time he was back at the Oakland Park Flea Market that was burgeoning with customers as the local high schools dismissed students. The hustle and bustle of competing for customers was a normal occurrence inside the flea market in which many vendors had various commodities for low affordable prices.

"I need a nice case for my phone. You think that will fit in here?" a fine woman in her early thirties asked pointing to a pink crystal studded case.

"I don't know let's check it out," Casanova replied. A complete showman as always Casanova was smooth with his hustle as the woman was infatuated by his calming aura.

"Looks like we gotta winner. A perfect fit," Casanova stated as the words seemed to roll off his smooth lips.

"It most definitely is," she replied subliminally flirting. Casanova caught on quickly playing into her fantasy because making money was his ultimate fetish and he needed her sale.

"Anytime you want to change it just slide it off."

"Or in for that matter," she replied delving into what she really desired.

"In sounds good too but it must be done correctly. Not too hard not too soft. Just…right," he seduced staring into her brown eyes.

"How about I leave you my name and number so you can get at me to see if your um' case fits my phone."

"I gotta warn you that I'm a businessman with bills to pay."

"And I'm a businesswoman so I can handle the expense. Just call me my name is Meka. Contact me at 754.567.8381. Make sure you holla sooner than later," she stated casually.

"Aiight my name is King and that's my number coming across your screen right now."

"Alright I got it," Meka replied giving him a soft round sight to see as she sashayed away making her butt slowly bounce enticingly. Casanova King just shook his head side to side as similar encounters with many gorgeous women were becoming the norm. As the sun continued in its unchanging orbit Casanova hustled and roamed around the flea market until about eight o' clock p.m. in which he shutdown his booth and dispersed the establishment.

Chapter 3

"Girl you mean to tell me you were at work with no panties on?" Monica asked laughing in disbelief while inwardly admiring the sexcapade.

"Yes the sex was so good that I wanted to do whatever he asked."

"Sounds like you dick whipped!" Monica exclaimed in a tipsy stupor.

"Yes chic I'll let him beat this good poonannie whenever, wherever," Lacy admitted giggling as her pussy twinged lightly at the thought of a future heightened orgasm. Monica and Lacy hung out at a bar in downtown Fort Lauderdale; Las Olas Boulevard to be exact, listening to the live bands while occasionally conversing about the most important issues to them--- men and sex!

"Hold down the table I need to use the restroom," Lacy remarked. Once Lacy was out of sight Monica reached inside Lacy's purse grabbing the cellphone searching for the number labeled King. Monica found it, stored it into her phone then placed Lacy's phone back inside the handbag.

"Girl I'm bout to get out of here before I get too drunk and can't make it home," Lacy stated as she came back to the table. Monica inwardly ruminated, *Chic you read my mind,* but instead she stated,

"Alright chic you be safe I'll be gon in a few," hugging her friend before she left. Monica had intentions to down a few more sex-on-the-beach drinks while devising a conniving scheme to get a sample of what Lacy continued to boast about.

"What's up mama?" Casanova asked simultaneously kissing his mother on the cheek.

"Nothing much. I was waiting on you to come by because your daddy called asking were you coming up to Atlanta for Christmas to see him."

"What you doing for the holidays?"

"I'm going to hang out with my aunt in Alabama," Ms. Brenda replied.

"Alright I'm juss checkin cause I ain't gon leave you by yourself."

"Boy I'm grown I'll be alright," she replied waving her son off. Casanova walked throughout the house going into a room he once occupied full-time. He still kept a lot of his clothing within because home was always home and he hadn't yet moved into a place of his own. Ms. Brenda occupied a three-bedroom home within the community of Melrose which was near the hood but still a nice distance from the hood how she like to live. In the meantime Casanova took a shower feeling the urge to freshen up for the evening. After the shower Casanova utilized his cellphone to organize a meeting with Meka as well calling Deja to see what she was up too. Casanova dressed himself in a army green pair of Tru Religion cargo shorts with a white Tru Religion tee shirt as the emblem matched the hue of the shorts. He reached into the back of the closet opening a Timberland box that contained a fresh pair of wheat colored construction styled boots. He wore them loosely stringed with white socks stopping just above the ankles.

"Ma I'm bout to go out. If you need me just call my cell," Casanova stated kissing his mother's cheek.

"Aiight be safe. I love you."

"I love you too mama." Casanova left out the house brushing his hair seeking to perfect his waves. As he pulled off Casanova thought to himself, *Man I hope this broad don't waste my time,* turning up the sound system bumping Drake featuring Young Jeezy; Unforgettable. Tameka Watkins lived alone in a two bedroom condo located in North Lauderdale where many of her neighbors drove expensive vehicles and were employed at high-end jobs. Casanova arrived impressed by his surroundings parking within the designated spot marked VISITOR aware of the sneaky tow truck drivers. Before he had the opportunity to knock on the door Meka was already at the threshold motioning him to come into the plush bachelorette pad. The interior of the condo smelled of a mixture of powder fresh Febreeze and soft scented burning incence.

"Lock the door behind you please," Meka instructed as she walked past the long fish tank having a seat on the comfy couch cushions. Casanova was temporarily mesmerized by the exotic array of fish swimming throughout the tank.

"The main attraction over here," Meka remarked giggling.

"Yeah you definitely a sight to see," Casanova responded gazing at her with a, *I'mma fuck you good!,* stare in his eyes.

"Come over and have a seat let me talk to you," Meka stated.

I kno dis chic got paper so I hope she don't try to size me like I'm low maintenance, Casanova thought as he casually walked over to the couch where she sat. Meka popped a bottle of champagne pouring them both a glass. They made a toast in which Casanova had no idea as to what but he obliged anyway raising his glass.

"Well you probably wondering to yourself, what the hell I do for a living huh?"

"What makes you assume that?" Casanova responded with a question evading a direct answer.

"I see it all in your eyes. So I'm not going to remain a mystery to you. I own a female escorting service named FLAVORED DESIRES which I initially started in North Carolina but the lure of the tropical weather caused me to flock down south."

"So you're an escort?"

"Just let me finish. And no I'm not an escort I only dispatch appointments out to the ladies that I employ. Initially when I met you I was only seeking a great fuck because of course a hard working woman like myself has needs too. Then when you mentioned you were a businessman it really piqued my interest in you even more as I had a epiphany. I have many female associates whom could use your sexual services if you decide to come on board and make some money. Of course to market you properly a sample is needed," Meka spoke.

"So you want me to slang dick and get paid doing it?" Casanova asked very blunt.

"I assumed you were already doing it on a lower scale so I figured if your sex game was good as I believe it is you should get paid top dollar."

"And what's top dollar?" he asked curiously.

"Anywhere from twenty-five hundred up to ten stacks a call. I'll send you all the customers and we split the profits sixty-forty your way," Meka replied. Casanova rubbed his chin contemplating the amount of money that could be made responding, "Alright I'm game," while tossing back the remnants of the champagne in the glass.

"Consider us partners then," Meka remarked extending a freshly manicured palm that was never met. Casanova King was already down between her zebra printed form fitting mini-dress head first pushing her black laced panties to the side as he began to fondle her clit with his tongue. Meka opened her legs wide while leaning her head back in bliss as King licked and sucked her into a much needed orgasm. He expertly slid out his shorts and boxers without taking his boots off. *Time to go to work,* he thought. As Meka glanced down below she stated, "Ooh shit we definitely gon make some money," noticing the length and width of his chocolate dick.

As Casanova stood up Meka softly exclaimed, "Yes gimme dat dick!" while rubbing her clit anxiously awaiting to be sexed properly. Casanova slid inside her pussy walls resting his palms on the back of the couch in a push-up position allowing her to stare down at his manhood sliding in and out her moist pussy.

"God damn dis dick good!" Meka purred through heavy breathing. Casanova then instructed Meka to turn around as her juicy cocoa brown ass cheeks were tooted up. As he slid in deep and slow from the back Meka moaned, "Aiigh, aiigh unh hunh!" Casanova sped up the pace of his strokes as Meka's ass responded like a loose rubber band.

"Yes! Give it to me," Meka yelled in heightened tones of ecstasy. Casanova kicked off his right boot raising his foot to the ledge of the couch while he raised Meka's leg gripping her thigh. This method allowed him deep access into her pussy as she enjoyed each thrustful stroke. Pausing momentarily Casanova backed up allowing Meka to turn around and suck his erect penis as if it was the Tootsie Roll Pop she was deprived of as a child. Meka was sucking his dick so good he had to have a seat on the couch because his legs got weak. Mekal got off her knees and skillfully began riding his dick reverse motorbike with her palms on the floor. She would occasionally bring her pussy lips to the tip of his dick twirling around the head then sliding back down without missing a beat.

"I'm bout to cum!" he alerted through a suppressed moan. Meka slid off and began sucking his dick wanting to taste him and her at the sametime while he exploded thick semen down her throat. Once they were equally satisfied he stated, "Let me use your shower?"

"Go ahead I'll bring you a towel," Meka responded. Casanova finally redressed in which Meka had a thousand dollars cash spread on the table with a FLAVORED DESIRES business card next to it to confirm business was legit.

"I appreciate you."

"No I thank you. We gonna make plenty money so be looking out for my calls," Meka shot back.

"Alright cool. Well I gotta few things to handle but I'll be around."

"Fa sho handsome," Meka concluded walking behind him locking the door.

Chapter 4

"Girl you did that."

"Dat right there," Deja responded speaking to a customer. Just as Deja was collecting payment Casanova was casually strolling through the door of the hair salon. Casanova was carrying a bag of food from Pollo Tropical with Deja's favorite dish. He came in kissing her lips lightly then sat down in her swivel styling chair. Deja wore a white tee shirt with some army fatigue cargo shorts, a white Miami Heat fitted cap on backwards with a crispy white pair of Air Force low-top sneakers. The LAVISH LOOKS BY DEJA apron was draped upon her front side hanging from her neck.

"What's up bae?"

"You already know on the grind as usual," Deja replied opening the box of food allowing the blackened chicken breasts, brown rice and steamed broccoli to arouse her tastebuds.

"Dats wassup. What you wanna do tonight?"

"I don't know probably catch a movie or something," Deja responded before chewing on a savory piece of chicken.

"Aiight I'm wit dat," Casanova agreed noticing from his peripheral vision that he was the center of attention within the salon full of ladies.

"Come to think of it, where were you last night?" Deja questioned.

"Over at the gambling house. I was breakin they pockets so you know it was hard for me to leave. It was too sweet."

"Um hmm. If you say so just make sho you come by the house later because I can't be cooped up in the crib on a weekend," Deja remarked.

"Don't worry bae I'mma be there. Anyway let me get back over to the flea market cause I got my shop open. This Arab dude watchin my business for me."

"Alright I'll call you when I close up my salon," Deja responded kissing his lips. Once Casanova left the premises Deja noticing all the nosy faces stated, "Y'all need to mind ya business," giggling lightly.

"Girl you stay wit a fine man," a stylist named Unique chimed in while doing a customer's hair.

"I guess you can say I'm blessed then huh?" Deja mentioned with a question while she flipped the flat screen television to B.E.T. hoping to catch a few music videos. Unique wanted to say, *Girl the way he walking like he carrying an anvil between his legs yeah you definitely blessed,* but instead stated, "Yeah girl you are most definitely blessed," knowing that further discussion about another woman's man was off limits.

Deja finished her meal as the next scheduled client was coming through the door.

"Give me a minute to wash my hands and I'll be right with you," Deja remarked walking towards a small office in the back. Minutes later Deja returned prepared to do what she was known for; extraordinary hairstyling. Deja was capable of making a mediocre woman appear to be the princess of a foreign country which always allowed her to maintain faithful clients--- they craved to be and feel beautiful. As the day came to a decline Deja and the remaining hair stylists cleaned up and shut down the salon. Deja climbed into her cotton candy pink Mercedes-Benz suv squatting on crome 26-inch rims dialing Casanova's phone number.

"What's up bae? I'm leaving now," she informed. Momentarily pausing Deja listened as she couldn't believe what she was hearing.

"I can't believe you doin this. You know what don't even worry about it. Go do whateva you gotta do I'll be alright." Soon as Casanova finished trying to explain Deja remarked, "Bye!" angrily ending the conversation. Never one to cry over spilled milk Deja still had intentions to go out and enjoy herself. Self-confidence she wasn't lacking as she considered herself a fine boss bitch whom was more than willing to show and prove top notch status. She rolled off as the setting sun in the western horizon emanated a blinding reflection off her rims.

LACED PANTIES

The moonlight reflection glittered across the Atlantic Ocean as Casanova stood atop the balcony of a high-rise hotel overlooking the Fort Lauderdale Beach ambience. He was referred to the exquisite suite for special services with a paying customer.

"King I'm ready," he heard from within the interior of the suite. The voice emitted from a 37 year old Caucasian woman whom appeared to be in her late twenties. She had the appearance of a young Pamela Anderson from her glory days on the Baywatch sitcom. Carla was her name and she was the wife of a wealthy businessman whom rarely gave her sex because he frequently traveled throughout the country and abroad. If he did give her any sex it would be terrible. Carla so desperately needed orgasmic fulfillment and if paying for it was the trick she was more than willing. Casanova never sexed a white woman but from the stories he heard he drew a conclusion of what they desired; hard black cock. As Casanova attempted to enter the suite Carla stopped him falling to her knees freeing his semi-erect dick. Sucking dick was a fetish since her college days that she hated to perform with her husband. Yet, seeing the hard chocolate dick before her eyes caused Carla's renown desire to instantly resurface. While she was slurping and twisting on Casanova's dick he appealed to her fantasy moaning in sex tones, "Ooh shit baby you the best," understanding the art of satisfying the customer. With a single finger Casanova raised her head up and she offered somewhat of resistance due to his dick tasting so good. Casanova leaned Carla up against the balcony with her ass tooted up. He began fondling her pussy while simultaneously rolling a Magnum condom upon his dick. They were on the 20th floor so the voyeuristic sexcapade aroused Carla even more. When Casanova slid into her wet pussy walls from behind she yelled, "Uhn hunh fuck me! Fuck me with that big black cock!" as she tossed her blonde hair over her shoulder staring back at him. When Casanova was pounding her with hard strokes her soft plump ass cheeks became a light red shade while his palm prints left pleasurable bruises on her ass cheeks with each slap. Carla loved the deep penetration that seemed so foreign to her over the last ten years. Casanova picked her up continuing to pound her pussy from behind carrying her into the room. He placed her on the bed as she rolled over on her backside legs spread wide open. Casanova admired her pretty pinkish-white shaven pussy that was glistening like polished jewelry because she was so wet. He pushed her legs behind her head causing her toes to touch the headboard and began ramming her pussy in an angry manner as if her forefathers were the slave owners that had his fathers on the plantation and this was his revenge. She was in a state of ecstasy where return was nearly impossible. Casanova pulled out and Carla began to fondle her clit rapidly which caused her to skeet cum like a water gun. Casanova removed the condom and begin masturbating as Carla begin sucking his balls lightly.

"I'm bout to cum!" Casanova uttered as Carla opened her

mouth wide anticipating the load of semen. Casanova shot cum all over her face and hair as she swallowed much as she could catch. Carla had numerous amounts of discretionary income and she was thirsty for more sex. The hustlers mechanism within Casanova succumbed to a few more hours of sex in every position Carla could fathom. Casanova was making money but losing a good woman---Deja,at the same time. The thought crossed his mind occasionally but was quickly subsided as he was having fun slinging dick and accumulating currency in the process.

Chapter 5

"Yes mamm we appreciate your business... okay you take care. Bye- bye," Lacy stated ending the call with a customer. After the call Lacy exhaled deeply then went and stood peering out her office window overlooking the downtown Fort Lauderdale traffic. She was sexually frustrated in more ways than one but had to curb her nympho desires because work paid the bills. Two weeks passed since her last sexual encounter in which first chance she received sexual urges had to be fulfilled. In the meantime she rested her leg on the window sill while recanting down memory lane. Unconsciously Lacy began to touch her pussy through the soft fabric her slacks were made from. A tap on the wooden office door brought her conscience back to the present moment. Lacy walked over opening the door for one of her co-workers.

"Hello Ms. Hankerson how are you?'

"I'm fine Mr. Dunn and you?"

"All is well. I just wanted to remind you to fax the paperwork to our offices in Tennessee before you leave," Mr. Dunn responded.

"Thanks a lot because I nearly forgot," Lacy admitted.

"No problem but uh you don't look so well. You sure you're okay?" Lacy thought to herself, *Damn is it that noticeable*, but grinned smugly.

"Yeah I'm cool."

"Well if you ever need anything and I mean anything just call me," Mr. Dunn propositioned placing emphasis on the statement. Lacy examined his physique honing in on his crotch thinking, *I know he got a lil dick but I might need him to get off from time to time.*

"I'll definitely keep that in mind," she replied batting her eyes showcasing the *Lash Bae© mink* lashes---*Queen edition.*

"Okay well try to get some rest when you get off." Lacy's conscience inwardly shouted, *Get some rest! Fuck that I wanna ride some dick!*

"Alright I will," Lacy concluded walking him towards the door closing it behind him. Lacy leaned her head back on the closed door exhaling her sexual frustrations while reflecting upon the man and hard chocolate penis of her desires.

"I'm trippin cause you keep saying one thang and doin anotha."

"It's just that I been out here paper chasin so you know how it be," Casanova responded.

"Yeah I kno how it be! You always lying to me like I'm one

of these lame bitches or sumthin," Deja replied angrily.

"Come on bae you trippin," Casanova remarked attempting to diffuse an oncoming argument. Deja glanced at her watch stating, "You know what I got an appointment comin' thru. I'm out here paper chasin so you know how it be. I'll holla at you later," walking inside her salon.

Casanova stood next to the rental car he was driving somewhat stunned but being just as stubborn he stated, "Fuck it!" hopping in the car driving off. Casanova was driving with no particular destination in mind listening to Soulja Slim featuring Juvenile, *'Unh I like it like dat, she workin dat back, I don't know how to act, Slow Motion for me....'*. Glancing down at his phone that was vibrating in his lap there was a number flashing across the screen that was unfamiliar. Curiosity forced him to answer anyway.

"Hello… Naw I don't remember you but now would be a good time to meet you… Yeah I'mma come thru right now," Casanova concluded. Casanova King drove to a small office building located on University Drive near the Home Depot plaza. The sign on the door read:

PARADISE INTERNATIONAL TRAVEL AGENCY.

The establishment appeared to be vacated by all employees until he noticed a fine honey-bronze toned goddess appear from a back office.

"Hello I'm Monica," she greeted extending a soft palm.

I never met this chic befo but she sexy as fuck tho, Casanova thought to himself as he shook her hand gently replying, "My name is King and I'm glad to meet you again," raising her hand to his lips kissing lightly. Monica instantly felt a surge of sexual electricity run through her veins as King's entire aura exuded confidence.

"The pleasure is all mine. Come back here to my office so we can talk there because I have a few things to finish up," Monica stated bending the truth as she locked the front entrance door. Monica wasn't worried about customers passing through and her only hired employee had gone home for the day.

"Since you are here I must be truthful. I swiped your number from a friend whom continued to boast about your sexual talents so I been lusting for a sample myself."

Trifling but whateva, Casanova ruminated.

"That's not a problem," Casanova responded as Monica walked past him having a seat on the edge of the oakwood desk. Understanding that after one good fuck session Monica would instantly become a regular dickmatized client, therefore he planned to perform in an extraordinary manner as if he was receiving big payout. Without any forewarning King began gliding his hands up her honey colored thighs raising the navy blue skirt up to her waist. He grazed his hands across her G-spot in a teasing manner removing her V-shaped laced panties. He brought them to his nose to get a whiff of how her pussy smelled. The arousing scent caused him to explore with tongue to satiate his sweet tooth craving. Monica was so horny due to his expert licking skills that she began to remove her blouse and bra to fondle her nipples as her pussy juices were dripping on the desk. She was feeling as if the freaky lioness within had been loosened so she allowed her dreadlocks to cascade down her back. As he stood King kissed Monica in the mouth while her juices flavored his lips tasting sweeter than she imagined. Monica reached down between his legs lightly tugging at his dick in dire need of the stiff flesh. King pulled the skirt off as she now only had on heels to complement her naked body. King helped her off the desk aggressively turning her around taking absolute control. He slid his ten inch dick within her pussy walls from behind as she submissively purred, "Oh.. my.. God...aiighh!" in a state of passionate ecstasy.

Casanova palmed her left ass cheek while lightly gripping a fistfull of hair stroking deep and slow as if he was a R&B crooner serenading her with each rhythmic thrust. He paused momentarily squatting down biting her ass cheeks lightly then began to lick her pussy from behind. He was in ultimate freak mode as he was sucking the interior of her ass cheeks so passionately that a visible hickey formed.

"Yes King you the man. Yes suck my pussy! Ooh King," Monica purred hoping the dream of bliss never ended. He came back up raising her right thigh atop the desk with her right heel propped on the oakwood canvass. He began penetrating Monica's super wetness deep and hard as his balls tapped her clit in pleasurable cadence.

"Fuck me! Yes take this wet wet King!" Monica screamed in ecstasy utilizing phrases that she didn't know existed in her normal vocabulary. Monica was now laying on her back with her waist hanging over the edge of the desk. Her legs were straight up in the air forming the letter 'I' as King worked his hips digging gently inside her pussy; left to right in alternating fashion. He spread Monica's legs allowing her to watch as his hard chocolate slid in and out while he fondled her clit in circles. Allowing her a chance to catch her breath King stepped back and began to slowly masturbate. Thrilled by the sight of his long thick black dick Monica got on all fours atop the desk and began devouring at least eight inches of his glistened hardness without gagging. While knowing a sensitive spot on most men, Monica focused on the tip of his dick sucking rapidly. As his dick began swelling in her mouth Monica continued slurping as warm semen was moistening her throat. She drained every drop of him from his penis. They both got dressed afterwards except Casanova told Monica, "You don't need any panties. Every time you think about this dick rub ya pussy and chant King ding-a-ling," while staring at her with tranced brown bedroom eyes.

Not even wasting time Monica yelled, "King ding-a-ling!" rubbing her still wet pussy anticipating and hoping for more rounds of hard dick.

"That wassup. But check it next time you wanna reach me call the number on this card and ask for the services of King," he mentioned placing a FLAVORED DESIRES card upon the desk.

"No problem because you worth every dollar."

"I'm glad to be able to fulfill your slippery needs," he responded kissing her on the neck.

"Aiigh," she hissed hoping he fucked her more.

"I gotta go but never be afraid to call gorgeous," Casanova responded in a seductive voice.

"I'll be calling very soon," she assured. Upon closing the door Monica went back into her office as her booty felt loose like a stripper that was skilled at gyrating her ass cheeks. Monica had the ultimate high that she prayed to the kama sutra gods to never come down from--- intoxicating sex on a heightened plateau.

Chapter 6

Not wanting to become negligent in his business caused Casanova to begin spending more time at his shop inside the flea market. Holiday season was in full-effect in which money was trickling down through the ranks of the shopping good chain in plentiful amounts.

"Wassup you gon cut me a deal on the case wit the money signs all over it?"

"Yeah juss give me fifteen dollars," Casanova responded knowing that the particular bargain would profit him eleven dollars. The young black dude reflected for a while as he scanned over the other cases stating, "Aiight check I'll give you twenty-five for two,". Casanova made a facial expression as if it wasn't a good deal just to keep the customer off balance before replying.

"Aiight I'll do it just for you. Which ones you want again."

"The money case and the Miami Heat one." Casanova placed the two cellphone cases inside a small grey plastic bag printing out a small receipt that read across the top NO REFUNDS, handling business on a official level. The money made was small but Casanova understood the analogy if crumbs making bricks, bricks forming houses in which houses eventually expand into mansions. Therefore the gratification he felt from making honest money was one that couldn't be explained. As usual he always spent money at the fruit stand purchasing a pineapple cup as well a favorite of his; a mango salad cup which consisted of sliced mango, vinegar, salt and pepper. On his way back towards the cellphone accessory booth the Arab dude whom owned the clothing booth remarked, "As salaam alaykum King,".

"Wa alaykum as salaam," Casanova responded in the proper salutation he was taught.

"You know you need to sale me the booth because I'm always watching it for you anyway," he jokingly propositioned but was very serious about the offer.

"Mahmoud you trippin this my baby right here. I ain't selling my spot , sale yo shit," King replied shooting back the offer so he'd understand that the statement was offensive.

"No harm intended. I thought you had other ways to make money since you hardly open up anymore."

"This my baby and I ain't selling," Casanova assured eating a spoonful of pineapples.

"Alright I'm sorry for even asking," Mahmoud mentioned ending the discussion. Throughout the course of the day Casanova profited roughly three hundred dollars. He was grateful but Casanova knew as a grown man with bills to be paid he needed more to maintain. He shut down shop thirty minutes before the Flea Market closed then called Deja to check up on her. Judging by the stiff tone of voice she was using he came to the quick conclusion that she didn't want to be bothered. So he didn't bother. He drove to his mother's residence to change clothes in hopes Meka would have an appointment for him. He felt as if selling his body was the lowest echelon he could fall to but a motto that was now a cliché to boost his morale stuck, *Hell a lot of women doing it so why not me? I need this money more than anybody.* For the love of money….!

"Girl you mean to tell me you had good office sex?"

"One helluva cocktale huh," Monica replied raising her apple martini for confirmation that what she revealed was truth. Monica purposely negated to reveal the pantie keeping segment out of the story because it may have possibly hinted at who beat her pussy up proper.

"I like that. Shit the way I'm overdue I'd fuck a random guy on one of these pool tables with everybody watching," Lacy responded in a sexually frustrated tone.

"Girl you crazy but come on let's get a round in," Monica suggested sashaying over to one of the empty pool tables. Upon placing her drink down on the edge of the pool table Monica alerted one of the employees that they needed balls and sticks-

-- for Lacy that meant literally! Neither one of the ladies were experts but they were able to maintain a decent game to relieve some of the pent-up estrogen.

"I dunno what it is. I've had other sex partners but this one particular guy seems to have some sort of mind control over me," Lacy remarked with the pool stick wedged in between her legs rocking side to side anticipating her next opportunity to shoot. Monica maintained an inconspicuous look like, *Chic I definitely feel you.*

"Or do you mean body control?" Monica remarked laughing attempting to conjure up some type of humor.

"Both," Lacy responded giggling taking a sip from her drink.

"So what you going to do about it?"

"I wanna become his sex slave but I can't because I got to keep my bills paid," Lacy remarked truthfully.

Girl I wanna suck his dick right now, Monica thought.

"Damn girl the dick that good?" Monica asked knowing for a fact that it was.

"Yes! Yes! Yes!" Lacy exclaimed nearly having an orgasm at the thoughts.

"Well I think you better get some dick before you explode," Monica replied laughing wildly while thinking simultaneously, *Shit I gotta get that good dick before I explode my damn self.*

"He won't answer my calls anymore," Lacy finally revealed sitting down sobbing. Monica consoled her friend while reflecting, *Damn I hope I don't start acting like that.* At that very moment Monica knew it was time to depart the bar and allow Lacy to get home before her emotions took her to the brink of sexual insanity.

Chapter 7

Another eventful evening at the flea market as Casanova shut down shop early with minimal profits. No sweat off his brow though because the escort hustle had been helping him accumulate substantial revenue. The time was approximately seven o' clock in which Casanova had called the LAVISH LOOKS BY DEJA salon phone that was answered on the third ring by Unique.

"Alright don't tell her I'm coming through," Casanova stated before ending the call. When he arrived at Deja's salon there were still a few clients inside getting the finishing touches done to the particular hairstyles.

"Wassup bae, how you doing?" Casanova greeted holding a bouquet of red roses.

"Don't wassup bae me! And no I don't want them roses. As a matter of fact me and you are done because if you can't find time for me I don't have time for you!" Deja yelled literally embarrassing Casanova within the establishment full of women.

"Why you actin like dat. You know I be at my shop most of

the time on the grind trying to make a way for myself."

"Listen you can keep doing that cause I don't want you," Deja stated angrily allowing irrational emotions to make her say something that she didn't really mean. Casanova stared around at the faces of the nosy women while placing the roses on the counter stating in a raspy voice, "If that's how you want it so be it. You could have at least called me to spare me the embarrassment," while walking out attempting to regain a bit of his dignity.

Unique stared on in disbelief that Deja had the audacity to diss him like she did. Unique was appalled by Deja's actions because in all actuality Casanova was trying to make a honest living without throwing bricks at the penitentiary. Many of the women were laughing with the feeling that Deja earned points for all independent women in the world. Inwardly Deja felt a bit of guilt because she broke her number one rule; involving strangers in her personal business. Unique checked the caller ID on the cordless phone storing Casanova's phone number into her cell vowing to call him and apologize for Deja's rudeness. Until the opportunity presented itself for Unique it would be business as usual inside LAVISH LOOKS BY DEJA salon because all over the world it's always known that no matter what the hustle don't stop!

"What up you alright?"

"Yeah nothing too major."

"Aight well talk to me I'm listening," Meka remarked.

"As for next week we gotta postpone all appointments."

"Why wassup something wrong?" Meka questioned.

"No nothing wrong. I gotta ride up to Atlanta to holla at my pops for the holidays," Casanova responded.

"Okay and that's understandable but if you down to make some extra money I have a few lady friends who would be more than willing to sample your goods," Meka remarked in a erotic enticing voice.

"I'm always down for the easy money but no more than two clients who will spend good please."

"That's not even a problem just call me when you touch down and I'll set everything up."

"Alright cool. I'mma head to the crib to get some rest cause I've had a long day," Casanova concluded headed to the door.

"That's fine but um when you're not so busy or tired don't forget about me because I'm feenin like Jodeci,," Meka teased.

"You a trip but I got you just let me catch up on my rest."

Casanova arrived at his mother's house which was empty because Ms. Brenda had already taken off to Huntsville, Alabama. Fatigue had engulfed him as he went straight into the room that he occupied since a youth flopping down on the bed dozing off instantly. He slept for a mere three hours but arose at two in the morning feeling well rested. Casanova stripped down to his boxers and ankle length socks going into the kitchen preparing himself a bowl of Cinnamon Toast Crunch cereal. While eating Casanova flipped through his cell phone's missed call log. No one really important to him at the current moment reached out. In the mist of eating and viewing a late night segment on ESPN SportsCenter Casanova received a call on his cell. *I don't know who this is,* Casanova thought as the particular number blinking on the neon colored cell phone screen was foreign to him but yet curiosity overtook rational judgment.

"Hello," he answered.

"Hey King how you doing?"

"I'm chillin but uh who this?" he inquired quizzically.

"Oh I'm sorry this Unique." Unique on the opposite end of the phone line was at home sitting indian style on her living room couch wearing some light brown laced boy shorts with a light brown navel length shirt that was embroidered with JUICY DRIPZ across the front in a darker brown hue.

"What's good Unique?" Casanova asked really wanting to say, *how did you get my number?* but differed knowing that women as well as men go to extremes when they want to find out something.

"Oh nothing much. I wanted to apologize for Deja's rudeness because the way she handled that situation wasn't right," Unique replied as she stretched out laying her head on the arm rest of the sofa.

"It's cool I ain't even trippin. Don't get me wrong I was embarrassed at first but once I got in the car and drove off a bit of my dignity returned," Casanova replied laughing adding humor to the matter.

"King you are a very handsome man and I was upset that she would even do that but if you don't already know I'll tell you that it was her loss," Unique mentioned. Casanova thought to himself, *Unique fine as hell. Kinda look like her and Esther Baxter could be twins. If she keep on flirting she definitely got me.*

"I appreciate that but truthfully you are a star in my eyes far greater than a dime. I always thought you were flawless but being that I was with what's her name I couldn't just come out and say what I wanted to ya digg."

"I definitely feel you," Unique replied touching herself as his voice was sultry and arousing like a phone sex operator. They continued to converse for nearly two hours pertaining to anything that came to mind. Casanova shied away from the topic of sex simply because he was a man of action more than just mere words. Plus he hoped that was not her only desire from him. They agreed to meet up later in the day first opportunity that Unique had in between midday appointments. Meanwhile Casanova headed to the shower in preparation to start the day off right--- so fresh and so clean, clean!

Chapter 8

The sun had yet to rise as Casanova was already on the move. He was draped in a white T-shirt with the designer logo embroidered in black stitching, a pair of black stain washed denim shorts with a pair of black low top shell toe Adidas. Deciding he'd accumulate a quick couple hundred dollars he finally returned one of the many calls from the previous night.

"Wassup you still home?" he asked as the call was answered on the first ring.

"Alright I'll be there in a minute to catch you before you go to work," Casanova concluded ending the call. He arrived at the gated Pompano Beach apartment complex within no time. Lacy opened the door wrapped in a huge white towel noticeably frustrated from the lack of good sex which Casanova easily detected. As he walked in Lacy mentioned, "King why you do me like that?" referring to his three-week hiatus.

"I just be a bit busy at my shop it's not done intentionally," he responded in a somewhat truthful manner. King stripped down naked intricately placing his clothes on the couch so they didn't get wrinkled. Lacy was so horny that she removed the towel exposing her nakedness commencing to sucking King's dick as if her life depended on it; which her future sex life did. King understood that she needed a good fuck so he bent her over as she gripped her ankles like an experienced cheerleader while he stroked deeply from behind. Her head was between her legs as she watched his dick rhythmically slide in and out her wet pussy while his sack hung and swung like a pendulum on a grandfather clock. Lacy felt so good that she wished to live her life in the particular sex position forever. King now allowed her to stand straight up on one leg with the other pointed at the ceiling while continuing to feed her body what she craved for; long hard black dick!

"Ooh King you in my stomach. Get this pussy!" she whined in pleasure.

Allowing a bit of relief King released her leg sliding slowly out of her pussy. He took her to the bed laying her on her back licking her pussy in an expert fashion. Lacy couldn't believe that a man was capable of making her feel so good sexually. He was licking and sucking her pussy in such a delicate manner that she moaned out, "Ooh! King I love you,". Upon hearing those words he instantly switched lanes. As King re-entered her wetness he ordered, "Grip your ankles," while her legs spread widely. King pounded hard gently rubbing her clit until he could no longer hold back exploding semen all over her body that Lacy commenced to rub on her flesh like lotion.

"Let's go shower because you got to get to work," he

instructed. Lacy did as told noticing that she had a little under two hours to get to her place of employment. Once they came out the shower King suggested that she wear the yellow laced v-shaped panty and bra set. He helped her get it on while standing behind her kissing lightly on her neck and shoulders. Lacy silently thought, *Damn I wanna call into work and kidnap his ass.* Once they were dressed Lacy remarked, "Follow me up the street to Publix so I can get some money out the ATM for you." Casanova determined that it was best to always keep Lacy on his line in case the endeavors with Meka ever folded. Therefore he'd always have some money coming in even if it was small change. Lacy's glossy countenance revealed her inward state of bliss. Lacy walked away from the ATM as the calf-length white dress that had tropical flowers scattered throughout swung lightly in the early morning breeze. Lacy handed him four crisp one-hundred bills. He kissed her cheek before she strutted off to her vehicle with a, *I just been fucked good!,* swagger.

Anotha day at the office, Casanova thought as he drove off headed to get something to eat before opening up his cell phone accessory shop at the Oakland Park Flea Market. The morning started off slow for Casanova as the majority the flea market customers were shopping for jewelry or various clothing items. Every so often he'd lure a straggler coercing them to purchase the cell phone accessories utilizing his gift of gab otherwise known as charisma. While sitting on a wooden stool behind the counter of his shop the vibration of his cell phone nearly caused him to jolt out of his seat.

"Wassup cutie?"

"Ev'rythang cool trying to see you. Where you at?" Unique asked.

"At the Flea Market."

"Alright I'm leaving the salon right now. I'll be through in about ten minutes," Unique replied.

"Juss call me when you get out front," Casanova concluded ending the call. He was already standing outside when Unique stepped out the red Infiniti SUV sitting on chrome 24 inch rims. Unique had on some hip hugging jeans that seemed to be painted on the way the denim clung to her curves. She had on a white T-shirt that read across the front:

BADD B#TCH!, in blue with some blue suede low top Nike Dunks sneakers. Casanova understood that she was casually dressed due to being on the grind doing hair in which comfortability was a must. Her hair was in a perfect wrap that maintained a shiny black gloss appeal. Unique approached Casanova planting a juicy kiss on his lips that shocked him but not enough for him to withdraw the embrace.

"Wassup wit that?"

"When I want something I go after it," Unique replied arousing him with her straightforward approach.

"Dat right there," Casanova commented with a smile.

"So what you doing later?" Unique inquired.

"Going to get my whip cleaned then I gotta start packing for my trip to Atlanta."

"That's wassup. How you getting there?"

"Driving."

"By yourself?"

"Yeah by myself. I'mma stay bout four days."

"You want some company in case you need an extra driver?" Unique asked standing directly before him lusting over his smooth lips.

"If you come you gotta meet my peoples. They cool as fuck so you'll like them," Casanova stated.

"Alright I'm down because I want to do some shopping up there anyway," Unique accepted lightly kissing his lips while wrapping her arms around his neck.

"That's wassup."

"Come on let's go inside because I wanna get me a mango salad. Plus I wanna see what kind of accessories you selling," Unique remarked.

"Get me one too." When Unique returned Casanova was engaged in a potential sale with a customer. Unique stepped behind the counter sitting on the stool eating the mango salad while savoring the aura of the ultimate black entrepreneur Casanova exuded. She had another appointment in an hour but for the meantime she hung like a lioness marking her territory that was hers to claim.

Chapter 9

"Pops what's up?" Casanova stated as he hopped out the SUV in front of his father's home in Stockbridge, Georgia. There were at least ten vehicles out front as his family was gathering for the holidays as usual.

"You already know I'm glad you came up," Casanova Sr. replied slapping five bringing his son into a shoulder embrace.

"Pops this is Unique, Unique this is my dad," Casanova stated formally introducing them.

"Nice to finally meet the man who King gets his good looks from," Unique mentioned.

"The pleasure is all mine," Casanova Sr. responded extending a hand for a welcoming greeting.

"Who all inside the house?"

"All your aunties and cousins. Your uncle them in the garage eating oysters too," Casanova Sr. replied with a smile.

"As a matter of fact y'all come on in so they'll know you're here. Plus I know everybody would want to meet your lady. Y'all a couple right?" Casanova Sr. asked for assurance.

Please don't embarrass me King, Unique nervously thought

LACED PANTIES

as Casanova replied, "Yeah Pops. Unique is my lady," in a proud manner knowing that Unique's beauty placed her in a league among the baddest women on earth.

Damn King you so fine and the way you took control solidifying us as a couple turned me on, Unique's conscience ruminated as they were walking into the house. When Casanova Sr. and Casanova Jr. entered the home the women went to yelling as if their nephew was some sort of celebrity. Everyone was spreading love as Unique was instantly embraced by the ladies. The women knew that if their nephew was with her then Unique had to be good people. Casanova had female cousins whom were very analytical of any woman he was with because they considered themselves dimepieces. If he was to bring any woman into the family she had to be a showstopper also no matter how superficial that may seem. That was simply the code that young women in his family abided by. By the time they made it out to the garage Casanova's uncles had the garage door opened up. There were at least seven of them hanging out eating oysters and telling jokes. Casanova allowed everyone to introduce themselves as they were all impressed with their nephew's status.

"Uncle Skeet shuck me one of dem oysters," Casanova remarked.

"You betta open it yourself," he replied laughing passing Casanova the oyster knife in which he was familiar with the process. He opened one oyster placing it on a Saltine cracker with a dab hot sauce before tossing it into his mouth. That one oyster turned into twenty more King gobbled down. Casanova Sr. was the life of a gathering as Unique noticed where King formulated his charismatic abilities. Eventually everyone began dispersing home or to hotel rooms to change clothes for a turned up outing within the Atlanta nightlife. Before Casanova could leave his Uncle Pat stopped him stating, "You got yourself a nice young lady nephew. Make sure you do right by her cause a good woman hard to come by,".

"You know I'mma hold it down unc."

"That's wassup. Aye but I ain't gon hold you up. I love you boy," Uncle Pat stated whom was always as smooth Casanova as desired to be.

"Alright love you too. I'll be back around tomorrow cause I'm going to cruise through the city tonight."

"Be safe nephew." When Casanova hopped in the driver seat of the vehicle Unique mentioned, "You wasn't lying your peeps got good vibes,".

"Always. I'mma slide downtown so we can check into the room my people reserved for me. We can change clothes, do a lil sightseeing and take some photos if you wit it."

"Hell yeah I'm with all that and some," Unique responded rubbing on his dick alerting him that she'd soon want some. Unique's presence had him horny as the known aphrodisiac; the oysters that is, heightened his desire for a sexual encounter. Casanova definitely had plans to give her a proper sexual introduction of his godly essence.

The temperature outside in the city of Atlanta had dropped down into the low forties as the sun set in the western horizon. Neither King nor Unique desired to go out into the chilly weather. They were equipped with the proper clothing but the warmth and comfort of the Westin Hotel was more appealing. Remaining true to his initial intentions King began to capture snapshots of Unique via digital camera. Unique was sashaying around the suite that was seventeen floors up overlooking the downtown Atlanta nightlife that was lit to perfection. She was covered in a snowflake white v-shaped thong panty and matching bra ensemble from the JUICY DRIPZ brand. Unique also wore some white open-toe stilettos that had expensive fur along the strap wrapping around her shins. The poses she was doing were very enticing. The one pose that took King over the edge was when unique placed her palms on the balcony glass with her ass perched up slightly while seemingly overseeing her kingdom. The photo couldn't have been more perfect capturing everything the city of Atlanta was all about as well the sexual attributes Unique embodied. King walked behind her handing over the camera squatting down between her thighs simultaneously. He began placing warm kisses on the inside of Unique's thighs before trailing his tongue up to her wet juicy pussy. He intricately licked every portion of Unique's juice box while holding her panties to the side. Unique's juices were so sweet and savory that King was under the impression that God moulded fruity peaches after the semblance of her G-spot.

"Umm hmm eat dat pussy daddi," Unique purred.

As King arose from a squatting position Unique captured a snapshot of his bare chiseled chest and erect dick that was visible once he slid out of the black gym shorts. Unique was clearly lusting for every inch of King's rock hard body. She slowly yet seductively slid out of the panties that were soaked in her own cum. King spun Unique back around with her palms on the glass while he penetrated her warm wet pussy; doggy style position. King was in no rush so his strokes were slow and meticulous. Unique leaned her head back kissing King passionately while each long-stroke entering her pussy seemed to be speaking sex volumes stating, *I want you to love this pussy.*

"Yes daddi! I love dat dick!" Unique shouted answering an un-asked question.

As King increased the pace Unique tossed her ass back meeting each thrust. King momentarily slid out of her lifting her up as she turned around. She placed her legs on his shoulders as he squatted and began fucking slowly in a circular motion intending to ignite pleasure sensations within every inch of her warm wetness. Unique bit him occasionally on his chest causing an arousing ecstasy. Unable to remain in a squatting position King went over to the edge of the bed never breaking stride as he sped up putting the pound game down within her tight warm pussy.

"Yes King this pussy is yours!" Unique moaned in sexual bliss. Occasionally he'd alternate the pace in which when King slow stroked Unique purred many truths.

"Ooh King I wanna have your baby."

King placed Unique on her side putting his palms on her

waist. As King deep stroked within the softest place on Earth her ass continued to jump into his lap rhythmically. Unconsciously King released a load of cum deep inside Unique's pussy because it was so good to him he didn't want to withdraw himself. Unique tightened her pussy muscles so none of his orgasmic juices seeped out. It was as if King was the Energizer Bunny himself because he kept going turning Unique on to her stomach putting the dick down the way only the real can do. Each rapid stroke caused Unique's ass to meet King's pelvic area making a clapping sound as if a third-party was inside the suite giving a standing ovation. The two of them complemented each other as the sex continued for hours in every position and nearly every portion of the room. Afterwards King did something that had been non-existent in his life lately and that was cuddle. The night was still young, 1 a.m. to be exact, in which King's mind had begun to contemplate on the money Meka said could be made in Fulton County. King eased out of bed going to take a hot shower in attempt to reclaim a portion of his energy. Upon calling Meka he was given the time as well directions to the spot where his service was to be expected. King dressed himself properly according to the climate then alerted Unique.

"Bae I'll be back in a lil bit," King stated kissing her lips.

"Alright be safe."

Due to King's frequent summer visits to Atlanta he was familiar with the geographical region, so locating the Buckhead Community townhouse on Dunwoody Drive wasn't hard to find. King was granted access through the gaurd gate thinking to himself, *Damn! Dis what I call livin lavish.* As he walked into the townhouse King was greeted by three beautiful chocolate goddesses. They were all dressed in a provocative manner awaiting his arrival as one of the ladies were holding a small inexpensive video camera. The three women had recently graduated from Spelman College and desired to live out their fantasy before venturing out as married career women. On the marble countertop was a $10,000 payment that solidified the deal. Performance at his highest sexual level was a must for King. He hoped the tape didn't leak out into the wrong hands only kept for their own personal pleasure. *If it do oh well I'mma perform like a champ just in case the world get the chance to see me slanging this good dick,* King thought inwardly in reference to anyone viewing the tape. The entire experience was new to King which aroused him even more as he was preparing to give the ladies some down bottom Florida dick to remember for all ages. Within hours he'd be out back into the hotel room with Unique ten grand richer.

Chapter 10

Casanova was munching on a large cup boiled peanuts allowing the tunes to mellow out his conscience as Young Jeezy rhythmically chanted over the beat, *All we do is smoke, and fuck,... all we do is smoke..smoke...and fuck....* Unique completed the latter half of the nine hour drive from Atlanta to Fort Lauderdale. Embracing the feeling of being home Unique emerged off the turnpike heading west on Sunrise Boulevard. Unique rented and upscale apartment in Sawgrass located within a gated community. Each of the apartments within the complex were equipped with a one-car garage which was the deciding factor for the monthly rent totaling thirteen hundred. She was a only child so her mother and father helped out with the living expenses despite her making a decent income at the salon to afford the residence by herself.

"You can put all those bags on the bed inside the room," Unique instructed as King came through the front entrance toting the many shopping bags and suitcases.

Casanova thought to himself, *Man I gotta step my game up,* as realization dawned on him pertaining to his living conditions.

Every woman that he was involved with was equipped with a plush pad to call their own. Of course his mother's home was decked out exquisitely but that's exactly what it was; his mother's home. He had been saving funds so instinctively his conscience told him to get his grown man on claiming a spot of his own. Casanova chuckled lightly while thinking, *King with no castle huh? How ironic. Tighten ya game up.*

"Bae I'mma holla at you a lil later."

"Alright King be safe. I'll be here juss chillin so call me if you need me," Unique responded. Casanova kissed her a temporary goodbye then drove to his mother's house. He stashed his earnings from Atlanta removing Meka's cut before leaving once again. The long trip caused many bugs to get stuck on his vehicle so Casanova stopped through the carwash to clean up.

"NEWPORT SHAWTY wassup?"

"Clean whips! You definitely gotta dirty one but I got you," he replied butting a cigarette.

"Do ya thang then," Casanova remarked having a seat in one of the plastic chairs enjoying the warm climate of South Florida's winter opposed to Georgia's freezing temperatures.

Casanova sat back watching the cars roll by enjoying the feeling of being home in his element. In the mist of people watching, Casanova noticed Deja pull into the gas station within the same lot as the car wash. The entire time Deja pumped her gasoline she peered at Casanova as to say, *Nigga don't even bring your ass over here trying to talk.* Casanova felt the vibe so he threw his hands up palms facing outward in a position of defeat. Deja hopped back into the driver's seat with added emphasis exuding a magnitude of swagger cranking her sound system up a few decibels.

I'm single again, back on the prowl, I thought it was perfect, I don't know how..., as Trina, Rick Ross, Lil Wayne and Plies permeated the sound waves on the Single Again remix. Unfazed by Deja's antics Casanova continued to chill out allowing NEWPORT SHAWTY to do a full detail cleaning on his vehicle. Afterwards Casanova climbed back into his tricked-out SUV and drove off towards Meka's residence.

"I heard about your performance in ATL," Meka remarked as Casanova stepped through her door.

"You know I gotta hold it down," he responded. Meka was dressed in some blue jeans, a tight white wife beater which her hard nipples were visible and a pair of blue and white Air Max 95 sneakers to compliment the attire. Casanova handed her four grand that she stored within a small safe in the room.

"I got a customer on standby for tonight if you're ready," Meka propositioned coming out the bedroom.

"Set it up because I definitely need the money."

"Alright I'll make sure I text you the info," Meka responded holding a motorcycle helmet underneath her arm.

"Dats your badd ass bike outside?"

"You know me I'm a pro at ridin," Meka replied seductively

approaching Casanova.

"Yeah you definitely know how to ride like a pro without falling off," he responded obliging to the tease.

"If I didn't have somewhere to be that dick would be mine."

"Well you better go before you don't make it," Casanova responded gripping her ponytail gently while palming her round ass simultaneously kissing her lips. Nearly forgetting she had to go Meka had her eyes closed in a moment of sexual infatuation until Casanova stepped back mentioning, "Come on let's go get to the money," lightly tapping her denim covered ass cheeks. Meka sat with her booty perched up on the Yamaha motorcycle and rode off slowly as Casanova drove behind her. Once they were out of the complex Meka popped-a-wheelie speeding off assuring Casanova that she was a seasoned veteran rider. Casanova shook his head smiling driving off in the opposite direction. He headed to his mother's home to await for Meka to send the necessary information while also contemplating the particular style of clothing the night might call for--- always wanting to leave a lasting impression in more ways than one.

Casanova was given instructions to park his car at the airport with in the short-term parking lot and await near the taxi pick up depot at 7 p.m.. At the precise time a Hummer H2 stretch limousine pulled up to the curb. The driver asked with the window partially down, "Are you King?"

Before responding he thought to himself, *Damn! It's rare to see a female limo driver. And fine at that!,.*

"Yeah I'm him." The female driver motioned for King to get in the back while the tinted window rolled back shut. He entered the exquisite limousine to the sight of an extraordinary Brazilian goddess. The evening was actually her 34th birthday which she planned to spend in sexual bliss. Marietta was the daughter of the founder of a franchise Sports Bar & Grill establishment initially founded in Miami Lakes. Despite her family's wealth Marietta was a rebel that loved to indulge in the wild side of life.

"How you doing beautiful?" King asked closing the door as a limo begin cruising off.

"Much better now that you are here." Marietta whom resembled the singer / actress Mya in every form especially her luscious lips was sipping a mixture of Alize and Ciroc which gave her slanted eyes are glassy appeal.

"I'm glad to cause an ease and relaxation to your body," King remarked. Marietta tossed the remnants of the smooth alcohol down her throat resting glass upon the bar console. Within moments Marietta begin unbuttoning King's pants pulling his semi erect penis out his shorts. Her jaws seemed to be like a vacuum as performing fellatio was her passionate expertise. While she was chowing down on King's dick he teased her moist pussy with two fingers underneath the silver glittery skirt. Unable to hold back any longer Marietta begin craving for King to get deep inside her. She spread her legs wide as King entered her slowly only jabbing the tip of his dick inside to prepare her for his girth.

"Ooh King fuck me!" she screamed in a state of nymphonic bliss. King obliged digging deep and hard holding Marietta's legs back with her toes touching the window. This was the ultimate definition of sex on wheels. King instructed Marietta to stand up on the couch and stare out the sunroof window. He entered her doggystyle taking Marietta to a voyeuristic state of bliss. His strokes were not hard only long, deep and pleasurable. To cars passing by it seemed as if Marietta was a tourist awed by the south Florida ambiance. They had no clue she was receiving the fuck of her life. Unable to conceal her desire for rough sex Marietta came back inside closing the sunroof yelling, "King beat this pussy up!" as he began doing exactly what she asked.

They rode around for nearly four hours having sex in every position that came to mind. There was a moment when Marietta rode King reverse cowgirl style as if she was a seasoned stripper while he relaxed sipping alcohol enjoying her booty-ful talents. Marietta was dropped off to her birthday party where her family; husband included were awaiting her arrival. King was compensated with five grand and promised to be called upon again. The limousine driver after enjoying the freak show returned King to the airport as the reality of normal life clouded his thoughts. He momentarily sat inside his SUV with his head resting on the steering wheel as a discouraging feeling of being a high priced male prostitute permeated his conscience.

"Man fuck all dat emotional shit!" King motivated himself ridding the particular thoughts from his mind. King tuned into the sounds of one of his favorite rappers in the game, *I'm out for presidents to represent me...Dead fucking presidents to represent me.....*

He paid the adequate parking fee as he departed with plans to go take a shower, renew his mindset then catch up with Unique.

Chapter 11

"How you been chic? I ain't seen you in a few weeks," Lacy remarked removing her shades having a seat at the bar.

"Been busy booking spring vacations for my clients," Monica replied in an exhausted tone.

"Speaking of vacations I could definitely use one right now."

"Vacation, sexcation it all sounds good right now," Monica agreed.

"Sexcation! Girl now that's definitely a ecstasy trip I want to go on," Lacy chimed in a cheerful demeanor. Motioning with a hand gesture towards the bartender Lacy ordered, "Two amaretto sours please,".

"So I take it you need some good sex in your life?"

"Do I!" Monica exclaimed while sipping her drink through a straw.

"So what we going to do?" Lacy inquired letting her friend know they were together on the issue.

"We gon find one if these dudes in here tonight and give them their ultimate fantasy," Monica insinuated.

"Girl you crazy," Lacy replied laughingly staring into Monica's eyes. Noticing that Monica was serious sparked the freak within Lacy so she remarked, "In that case you pick him out," as they began the hunt staring at the bulges in the crotch regions of the men at the bar. The lack of good sex caused their mind to venture into a domain that was unfamiliar to them. Their minds seemed to lock in on the same plane of thought as Monica held up her glass for toast, "One life to live!"

"Might as well enjoy him!" Lacy conceded as they were preparing to proposition to the man they had zeroed in on.

"Ooh I can't stand him!" Deja stated inside her vehicle as she made a U-turn. Casanova zoomed by on 441 negligent to Deja whom was a few cars back following him. Deja had no real mission in mind. Her emotions running rampant were the driving force behind her trailing him. Casanova was bobbing his head to the tunes of Rick Ross' *Aston Martin Music* as he recently shut down his shop at the flea market and departed into the streets. He only accumulated $200 but despite the minimal amount it was better than being trapped in a metal hell known as prison. When he halted at the light on the intersection of Broward Boulevard and 441 Casanova noticed Deja's pink Mercedes Benz SUV a few cars back apparently following. First thought came to his mind was, *I should send her a text and tell her that if she wanna talk we can,* but he deferred. The light turned green as Casanova took off, quickly making a left turn into the Melrose community while Deja continued to travel straight merging onto the Northbound Turnpike on-ramp. Casanova shook his head horizontally as he parked at his mother's residence going inside thinking, *It probably was just a coincidence,* pertaining to the sighting of Deja's vehicle.

"What's up ma how you doing?"

"Fine. About to head over to the hospital and put in some overtime," Ms. Brenda replied as Casanova kissed her cheek.

"Cause we out here grindin!" Casanova playfully shouted.

"Boy you crazy. Make sure you lock up my house if you leave," Ms. Brenda reminded laughing at her son's antics.

"You know I will ma don't worry."

"Alright I'll see you later. Love you."

"I love you too ma," Casanova replied walking his mother out into the garage. Once his Mom left Casanova closed the garage simultaneously dialing Unique's number on his cell.

"Wassup bae you home?" he asked pausing awaiting an answer.

"Alright I'm getting dressed now I'll be through in a little bit," he concluded. After a brief shower Casanova dressed himself and a smoke gray Lacoste short sleeve polo shirt with the emblem all black, a pair of black denim shorts that were creased to perfection, complemented by an all black and gray pair of LeBron James sneakers. And black digital glow-in-the-dark Lacoste watch was wrapped around his left wrist as the same brand cologne was sprayed upon his flesh. When Casanova arrived Unique called his phone instructing, "Bae park your car in the garage we gon take my car,".

Just as Casanova parked his vehicle Unique was slowly coming down the steps in some exclusive black leather stiletto platform pumps that strapped below her ankle. Her body was wrapped in some black denim skinny jeans that accentuated her curvaceous figure and a black satin shirt that did well for her cleavage. Her hair was cascading down her back with honey brown colored streaks arrayed throughout. Unique had an assortment of diamond jewels on her shining like the Eastern Star. Casanova approached kissing her glossed lips as she said, "Bae you can drive," handing him the keys.

Before they got in the car Unique remarked, "King let's take a few pictures before we go," removing her iPhone 5 out her small baguette purse. They traveled down to Miami's South Beach strip to eat at Prime 112. The entire time they trekked Southbound on Interstate 95 an array of sultry R&B jams mellowed out their mood. After their meal the couple decided to join the star-studded nightlife where they fit perfectly like symmetrical pieces to a jigsaw puzzle. Club LIV was loaded with celebrities on this particular night as Casanova was saluting many of the street legends that he knew. He always wanted to pay homage to the real niggas. Two and a half hours of partying along with a few drinks to support before the couple exited the lure of the glitz and glamour making the trek back north to Broward County. When they returned to Unique's place of residence sex between the couple was inevitable as their bodies had an invisible magnetic attraction. Casanova made it a top priority to please Unique at the highest pinnacle he could accomplish. Reason being is that Casanova wanted for Unique to embrace every facet of her sexual prowess. Also the vibrant sex methods Casanova used were for added assurance that he was down for her no matter what rumors the streets would soon conjure up. For the meantime all was well for the couple but Casanova always prepared for the gossip because the Fort Lauderdale streets would always be tough on a playa on the rise to personal greatness.

Chapter 12

"Yeah girl I don't know what I was tripping on. The dude still stay with his mama," Deja remarked laughing.

"I don't know Deja at least he ain't selling drugs," Unique chimed in while doing a client's hair.

"You got a point but there's still a time when a man must step his game up. And guess what? he ain't doing that!" Deja continued causing all the women inside to nod in agreeance. Unique wanted to reveal to Deja that Casanova was her man now but instead she continued to listen. Unique was intrigued that her man was the topic of the evening.

"I hate these dudes that ain't bossin up. I followed him the other day just to tell him that he ain't shit but I never got the chance to tell him," Deja conceded in an angry tone.

"I mean a boss had to build up to that status. We as black women must learn to support our black men a lil better. You know help them reach that status. You did say King owned a booth inside the flea market right?" Unique stated already knowing the answer to her question.

"Yeah he do."

"Well he's elevating himself and prison don't seem to be his destiny," Unique continued.

"I guess but it don't matter no more cause I ain't got time for this trifling no money getting ass anyway," Deja replied.

"We gotta destroy the stigma of all black women being so-called gold diggers," Unique shot back.

"Whatever. It is what it is these no good black men especially King need to get they shit together. Simple as that," Deja responded gaining the excited approval of all the women inside the salon. Unique never replied even though she was fuming mad. The female clients enjoyed the open opportunity to bash a black male that possibly had the utmost respect for them. No longer wanting to hear the fruitless black male bashing conversation Unique picked up her cell phone.

"What's up bae?"

"Juss coolin. On my way back to the Flea. I had to go pick up my keys to an apartment I got approved for in Inverrary," Casanova replied while his cell phone was on speaker resting in his lap. Unique thought to herself, *And these raggedy bitches was just talking shit about him. What a coincidence.*

"That's wassup. I had you on my mind so I was just checking on ya."

"You already know me. Steady on my grind trying to make a way."

"I love that hustla's ambition about you not to mention ya um good love making skills too," Unique responded laughing attempting to remain discreet due to the ear hustling women inside the salon.

"Thanks for the compliment but truthfully your pussy is so good it brings the best out of me," Casanova shot back feeding into the midday foreplay stroking her ego.

"Ooh bae you better quit before I come get you right now," Unique warned blushing.

"Aiight, aiight I will but just know dat you a star in my eyes. Can I be politically correct and say you are badd chic?"

"Yes I'm definitely a bad bitch," she said in a swaggerific tone.

"Alright dat right there. But bae lemme get back inside the Flea Market and handle up. I'll see you a lil later tho."

"Okay my love I'll catch you later."

"Love," Casanova concluded ending the call.

"Chuck what's up with Mahmoud? I ain't seen him open up shop in three days. Something wrong?" Casanova asked the man who was in charge of renting out booths within the flea market.

"Man this dude was pushing so much cocaine it'll make your head spin. The F.E.D.S. indicted of his entire family, women and all. It was all over the news so I thought you knew," Chuck replied.

"Naw man I've been kind of busy so I haven't been able to

catch the news."

"I gotta try to sell all the property inside to get my rent money for this month."

"How much is the rent?"

"Seven-hundred dollars."

"How about I take over the rent and continue to run the clothing shop?" Casanova propositioned.

"If you can handle it go for it but the money must be on time every month," Chuck advised.

"Have I ever been late with payments?"

"No you haven't. Always precise with business," Chuck admitted.

"Alright then know that we have a deal. Don't worry about anything," Casanova concluded shaking the Caucasian man's clammy palm solidifying the deal.

"Deal. I'll have the contract printed up by Monday."

"No problem." Casanova was elated feeling as if he was finally granted the opportunity to corner off a piece of the flea market's daily money flow. *Hell the Chinese people doing it every day opening a hair salon, beauty supply store and a nail salon all in one section,* Casanova thought inwardly reflecting on his monopolizing abilities.

Chapter 13

"Ooh King I want you to do me like dat," Meka purred while watching the video of King and the three women from Atlanta. Shaking Meka from her sexual trance was her ringing cellphone on the table.

"Alright I'll be there in a few," Meka concluded ending the call. She paused the DVD as the moans, purrs and fuck me's from the women came to a halt. Meka put on some jeans, a form fitting wheat colored tee shirt with the words *BIKER CHIC* across the front with a pair of wheat colored Timberland boots covering her feet. Within ten minutes Meka was on her Yamaha heading southbound on Interstate 95 occasionally reaching speeds topping 100mph. Meka pulled the motorcycle to a stop in the parking lot on Fort Lauderdale Beach lightly revving the engine twice for good measure before shutting it off. Casanova whom parked a few spots down in a rental car approached the motorcycle as Meka was removing her helmet.

"Come on put your helmet in the car," Casanova remarked leading her towards the rented vehicle. Before taking a stroll down the beach shore Casanova stopped by the automated payment machine. On Fort Lauderdale Beach it was a must to pay for parking if not it was impossible to prevent the towing company from quickly confiscating the vehicle--- very sneakily at that!

"So wassup?" Meka questioned as they casually strolled down the shoreline.

"Juss vibin. Juss thought it would be cool to hang out with the boss lady," Casanova replied inwardly gauging her reaction.

"Is that what it is?" Meka asked laughing lightly.

"Somewhat. Truthfully I really wanted to tell you that in three months I'm getting out the business."

"Why is something wrong?"

"No nothing is wrong. I just don't feel if this lifestyle this is for me," Casanova replied having a seat in the sand barely visible to by-passers.

"I need you. The ladies have been calling for your services a lot lately. Your value has increased tremendously so please just give it a little more time. We could become multi-millionaires in nearly a year," Meka informed.

"Millionaires huh?" Casanova reflected.

"Yes baby. I've been negotiating with some top notch clientele whom I know will spend adequately."

"Well if you put it like that I'll ride out a lil longer and see how the money rolls in."

"Don't worry soon you'll be making so much money ya head gonna start twirling."

LACED PANTIES

"Sounds good to me cause I definitely need it."

"You gon get it but um you know what I need?"

"Gon ahead and get what you need then," Casanova responded licking his lips enticingly. Meka wasted no time bending between his legs pulling his hard dick out. While Meka sucked his hardness in a craved manner Casanova held the back of her head, strongly aroused by the slurping sound. Pausing momentarily Meka removed her boots and jeans desiring to be fucked real good--- ghetto voyeurism at its finest and sexiest. Casanova was in full control as Meka was on all fours staring back at him while the full moon's illumined reflection shimmered within her lustful brown eyes. Casanova was immensely aroused as he slid his dick within her pussy doggystyle gripping her panties by the waistline, simulating riding a bucking bull. The entire ambiance was soothing which the only sounds were of the waves crushing against the soft shore and the intense moans of pleasure released from Meka's vocals. Casanova allowed Meka to get on top and ride his dick in fluid motions as if his dick was her Yamaha motorcycle. As Meka was grinding and bouncing atop his dick Casanova would occasionally slap her booty cheeks with a Sandy palm. The friction of the fine grade white sand caused an erotic sensation with each slap issued. With a continuous stroking momentum Casanova flipped Meka over on her back as if they were an adept wrestling duo.

"Ooh King beat this pussy up good!" Meka yelled as her

legs were up in the darkened sky.

Damn bae sex game official, Meka thought as Casanova stood her up and entered her pussy from behind raising one leg up stroking with a constant rhythm. The particular position caused her to climax hard.

"Aiiiiggh!" Meka moaned while leaning her head back kissing his lips lightly as her legs were pleasurably weak. Meka wanted to say, *King I love you,* but her words were caught up as Casanova had his left hand gently wrapped around her throat. When he released the light grip Meka exhaled a deep sex breath stating, "Aiiiigghh! King this pussy is yours," while he climaxed simultaneously within her warm walls of ecstasy.

King never responded because Meka's wet body language already confirmed what she voiced. They got dressed and ventured back towards their vehicles with Casanova carrying Meka's sandy body on his back. They could care less if any nosey people watched their outdoor sex performance.

"Call me when you make it home," Casanova instructed as dropped Meka off to the motorcycle.

"Alright daddi I will," Meka responded with love and lust emanating from her pupils.

"Cool. Don't give my pussy away," Casanova remarked cupping her ass kissing her succulent lips simultaneously.

"It's yours baby. Now let's get full because the money out here for the taking."

"Dat right there." Casanova handed Meka her helmet then

watched her slowly ride off under the moon. Across the street at the local bar Lacy and Monica witnessed the occurrence.

"Girl is that King right there?" Monica asked in a jealous yet lustful tone.

"Yep that's his good dick as but um how you know him?" Lacy questioned in return with a quizzical stare down.

"Oh yeah I forgot to tell you about this client of mine that gave me a card to a male escort service and he was referred to me for sexual favors...," Monica replied fabricating how she initially encountered King. The entire time Monica was explaining Lacy inwardly ruminated, *Bitch you ain't shit and I know you lying. If you wasn't my homegirl I'd kick yo ass. But fuck it!, cause I can tell by the way ya leg twitchin dat ya pussy itchin for some dick from King and we gotta common goal so we gotta work together wit ya triflin ass.*

"Enough of the bullshit Monica I forgive your conniving ass. You want his dick and so do I so we gotta figure out a way to get him to eat out of our hands," Lacy remarked very straightforward.

I can't believe the nerve of this bitch even though she is right, Monica reflected.

"So what you wanna do? Follow him home, tie him up and take the dick?"

Chic you crazy!, Lacy thought.

"No we can't do that and you need to stop watching that crazy shit on Lifetime. Whatever we do it must be done right,"

Lacy stated with realization of their careers in mind. Lacy sat frozen momentarily with her drink seemingly glued to her right palm plotting a scheme very meticulously. Casanova drove away from the beach unaware that he was in the human crosshairs of two sex deprived dick junkies. Smart women with an ulterior motive were always a true playas worst nightmare. Casanova turned up the knob on the rental car's radio system a few decibels bobbing his head as the music permeated the ambiance within.

My bitch badd lookin like a bag of money....she badd badd... .

Another day another dollar was the motto for most hustlers but in King's case it was another orgasm another stack of money.

Chapter 14

"Yeah I'm comin thru right now. I ain't gon be long tho cause I gotta get back to the shop," Casanova stated ending the call. Casanova was initially hesitant to go through the salon but differed upon realization that he and Deja had moved on with their lives. When Casanova rolled his Escalade into the parking lot Unique was already outside awaiting his arrival.

"Fried rice, sesame chicken with a few fortune cookies on the side," Casanova stated jokingly with a imitation Asian accent.

"Bae you a trip," Unique replied smiling widely while retrieving the small bag with the food inside.

"Yeah you know trippin over you wit ya sexy self."

"Check you out. Do me a favor please and take my car to get washed when you leave the flea market later if you can?" Unique suggested.

"Aight well if I'mma do that we might as well trade whips now," Casanova remarked.

"Here go my keys."

"Alright give me a minute ," Casanova replied properly

backing into one of the empty parking spots. Upon handing Unique the keys Casanova kissed her lips stating, "I'll catch up with you later iight," while staring at her as if she was the only woman in the world that mattered to him.

"That right there baby," Unique concluded equally gazing into his eyes in the same demeanor. Unique walked back into the salon as the unusual silence is exactly what she expected. Deja still wanted Casanova in which her menacing stare at Unique said a million words without a sound. Unique played the tension to the left and began eating her lunch awaiting two scheduled appointments. Deja would address the issue as soon as the opportunity arose which was possibly minutes away. Minutes transformed into tension filled hours before Deja spoke to Unique.

"Unique how could you do that? I thought you were my friend."

"Deja I'll always be your friend true indeed but he's a good guy. You said you hated him so I figured I'd give him a try."

"Friends don't mess wit each others man Unique."

"I guess you forgot how you dissed him in front of everybody plus you talked about him like a dog but yet you still say he's your man. Deja you really are selfish," Unique responded coolly understanding that they had to work together but more importantly Deja was the salon's CEO and her boss.

"I can't believe you. You of all people know that I love him and that I was only blowing off steam."

"Dejanae you've changed and despite you trying to blame this on me you brought it upon yourself."

Deja never responded because deep down she came to the conclusion that everything Unique spoke was absolute truth. *Truth hurts and love kills slowly,* Deja silently thought to herself walking back into her office space.

And it kills me……to know how much I really love you…..so much I wanna ooh ooh ooh…to you ooh ooh…. The particular song by Melanie Fiona permeated throughout Deja's car interior as she drove away from her salon for the evening. Deja's mind reflected upon a million and one different thoughts.

I wonder if he loves her?..., Does he still love me?..., How did I let him get away?...,Damn I didn't handle that right!..., Deja you did some dumb ass shit exposing his business to dem broke ass bitches in da shop that can't even keep a piece of a man.... Deja never exposed her private life to the public especially amongst clients in which lately she seemed more than willing to air her life out to any available listener. Focus had to be regained in which she was determined to realign herself with the real Deja.

Deja get yourself on point and back to what's yours if you want it, her conscience ruminated. At the current moment Deja was driving towards a 24-hour tattoo parlor that she was familiar with. The tattoo artist at the particular shop had a divine ability to identify with the desires of customers roughly illustrated thought. Every since the initial ink had been inscribed within Deja's skin the particular shop had become a comfort zone to her whenever she was feeling the need to record life's journey.

"What's up Deon?" Deja asked as she entered the parlor.

"Been waiting on you," the buff tattooed black guy responded with a proper speech edicate.

"I'm here. What you come up with," Deja asked exhaling deeply.

"Something special. I believe you'll like it," he remarked showing her a huge mural sketched on drawing paper as the underlining theme was, *LOVE KILLS SLOWLY.* Deja was definately impressed by the vivid images of how her entire back would look upon completion which caused a tingling sensation to travel throughout her body.

"Give me a minute to go outside and get my IPad," Deja uttered.

"That's cool because I need a lil time to get prepared anyway."

Deja returned inside five minutes later with her iPad and Beats by Dre headphones zoned out to Lil Wayne featuring John Legend; So Special. Her eyes were glossy and she done something that wasn't done in a while---smoke a blunt of high-grade. Only reason she puffed the marijuana was to relax her muscles as well free her mind from the pain of getting a tattoo. Deja lay comfortably on her stomach shirtless as Deon skillfully went to work inking her entire back piece incorporating various colors where needed. Occasionally Deja shed a few tears that rolled down her cheeks dripping to the black and white checkerboard tiled floor. Each tear that fell told a story within itself that would forever be unheard. The tears were not really from the pain of the needle but moreso from the pain in Deja's heart because to her it was true, *Love does kill slowly.*

Chapter 15

The weeks had turned into months as Casanova had definately stepped his status up to another plateau. He had decked his one bedroom townhome out with plush furniture along with various luxury amenities. Due to his flea market establishments as well as his extracurricular hustle going well, a nice lump sum of cash had began to stack up in his small safe. Life was good for Casanova. Despite it pouring down raining outside money was calling and that was the single most important job on his to-do list. Casanova hopped into his SUV driving amidst the torrential rain against his own right-minded judgment. The heavy rain pellets were crashing atop the roof of the vehicle in loud thud noises while the windshield wipers rapidly moved back and forth. Lightning streaked throughout the sky as thunder followed behind in loud bursts. Seemingly spared by divine intervention Casanova was halted at a red light while a major three-car accident occurred before his eyes. *Damn that could have been me,* he thought. Upon witnessing the metal pile up with inevitably dead bodies trapped within Casanova instantly had a change of plans. *The streets ain't safe right now,* he ruminated placing a call on his cell phone.

"Unique, baby you home?... Alright I'm on my way," he remarked ending the call. Immediately upon ending the call he made another.

"Meka baby cancel that appointment because driving out here right now is too dangerous. I just witnessed a bad ass accident and that shit spooked me a lil bit."

"Alright bae I'll take care of it. You be safe out there. I love yo handsome ass," she replied.

"Cool. Daddi love you too girl," he conceded ending the call. Casanova made a right on Sunrise Boulevard traveling west driving slowly taking all precautions because power was out causing all streetlight intersections to have the caution lights blinking for travelers of all directions; sometimes more dangerous than ever! Casanova refused to become a victim of slippery roads before arriving to his wet and slippery gorgeous destination.

"He cancelled!" Monica exclaimed dropping her cell phone on the oakwood table.

"Just have patience we'll get him," Lacy assured calmly.

"Yeah you right," Monica remarked laying her half naked body next to Lacy on the bed.

"Christopher come in here and take care of your masters!" Lacy yelled in a seductive tone. Christopher Dunn emerged into the room wearing Speedo briefs with a mini tuxedo imprint on the crotch region. He was nowhere near an adonis which the excess of furry chest hair solidified that. For the meantime he would suffice as the two ladies manipulated his mind transforming him into their personal sex slave.

Take me anyway you want as long as I can continue to taste yall good pussy, Christopher thought as he approached the bedside ready to serve. Lacy and Monica had emerged from their shells sexually as they were side-by-side kissing each other passionately while fondling each others pussy and breasts. Christopher kneeled between Lacy's legs as she gripped the chain dangling from his neck tugging his face towards her pussy lips. He instantly obliged like a thirsty nomad in the desert seeking the Water of Life. Monica climbed atop Lacy's face grinding her pussy against her tongue and lips while Christopher had two fingers jabbing in and out of Monica's tight asshole. The trio had encountered many sexcapades over the last two months as Christopher was not what the women truly desired. They utilized him for their ulterior motives that would take place in due time. After the mediocre sex that always left Monica and Lacy thirsty for some good dick, they redressed in their casual business attire to remain within the image of the normal hard-working citizens. The truths of their private encounters were never to escape their places of residence for the sake of their careers and family chasteness. Lacy was now confined behind the shield of her car's tinted windows as she began yelling out, "I need some good dick bad like a heroin junkie needs a fix. King you need to answer your fucking phone for me!" banging her palms on the steering wheel as she was taking off out the driveway. Monica was also frustrated shouting within her vehicle as well.

"Ooh King I hate you! You good dick bastard!" Monica vented pulling off behind Lacy's automobile. Inside the home Christopher peered out through the vertical blinds stating to himself, "I love y'all good pussy bitches. I'll do anything for y'all no matter what," while simultaneously puffing a Cohiba cigar with a silk black robe opened draped upon his naked flesh.

Damn y'all just left and I need more, Christopher thought while grabbing his miniature size dick unaware that he was pussy whipped by two master manipulators on a mission to get unlimited orgasms from the man that was constantly on their mind.

Chapter 16

"For that entire set just give me sixty dollars," Casanova stated referring to a Coogi shirt a customer wanted.

"Aiight dats a bet cause dat shit go good wit these kicks," the customer replied opening a black shoebox.

"Hell yeah! Dem thangs hard!" Casanova remarked with a great understanding of how to relate with customers. Casanova went behind the register cashing the guy out whom appeared to be a street hustler and his mouth full of gold teeth and large knot of one dollar bills exposed the possible profession.

"Alright playa you be easy and come back thru to holla at me," Casanova remarked.

"Say less," he replied walking off. The sun was nearing the midday pinnacle in which the normal crowd of customers had yet to come through the flea market to shop. Staying in tune with his normal routine Casanova had a seat on the bar stool in front of his clothing store. Seemingly appearing out of thin air, Deja's angelic presence was right before Casanova's eyes.

"Can I speak with you for a moment?" Deja asked calmly.

"I don't want no problems with you," Casanova uttered

holding his palms up.

"I come in peace."

"Cool we can talk inside my shop."

"I don't want everybody to hear," Deja remarked.

"I gotta small office inside just big enough for both of us." Upon stepping into the small quarters Casanova asked curiously, "So what's up?"

"Fist and foremost I want to apologize for everything especially the way I treated you in the salon that day."

"Ain't no pressure. I know you were venting all your frustrations with me."

"You don't have to down play it because I know I was wrong. But anyway I wanted you to know that my feelings for you have yet to go away. I love you still and I can't even lie. I know I forced you into other arms and I'm sorry. I came here to ask you in person if we could at least be friends again?" Deja stated nearly in tears.

"Deja I'll always be a friend to you no matter what. I never intended to be without you and there's always times when I'm like what if ya feel me. Anytime you need me juss call. Ain't nothing changed wit me but the date cause it's not easy to turn off the emotions of love. With that said hold ya head up because you are a very beautiful woman. Very delicate to me like a precious rose," Casanova responded pulling her into a warm embrace lightly kissing her forehead. Deja rested her head on his chest thinking, *He said that he still loves me. Claim ya spot girl!* Exhaling deeply Deja smiled remarking, "Thank you for always being so understanding. By the way when did you get this clothing shop?"

"You know me, ev'ryday I'm hustlin, hustlin, hustlin," he replied laughing.

"Well I gotta get back to my salon but I'll give you a call later."

"Aight cool. You be easy bae," Casanova responded as Deja surprisingly kissed his smooth lips lightly.

"Always you know me," she remarked sashaying away putting an extra ounce of sway in her hips keeping Casanova momentarily mesmerized. Casanova broke free of the daze instantly shifting gears into grind mode without a second thought. The day came and went as usual with a profit of six hundred dollars which was a decent amount to a black man who knew how to save money. The cellphone accessory shop wasn't doing so well and as a smart businessman Casanova was contemplating selling the lot to a small time fragrance dealer. More than likely the fragrance dealer would rush into the opportunity for better positioning towards the front of the Flea Market. Only time would tell but in the meantime Casanova was headed home to stash his earnings and check in with Meka to see if she had anything for him.

You can run the streets wit yo thugs, I'll be waiting for you,

LACED PANTIES

until you get through I'll be waiting....., were the sounds of the Tupac hit permeating the ambiance of Unique's residence as she opened the front door for King. Unique was instantly aroused as King's aura exuded everything that amounted to being smooth. As much as she was aroused by him, the feeling tingling down in his boxers was mutual. Unique had on some lavender colored boyshorts with a lavender navel length tee shirt with JUICY DRIPZ inscribed in purple stitching across the front.

"What's up babygirl?" he asked kissing her Alize´ flavored lips.

"Juss vibin like a badd bitch supposed to. You missed me?"

"Did I?" he responded always willing to feed her ego.

"How much?" Unique teased stepping up to him with her arms around his neck--- while her warm pussy rested atop his thigh.

"Girl I been having fantasies about me and you."

"About what?" she seductively probed.

"I'd rather just re-enact what I visioned," King replied raising Unique into his arms holding onto the cup of her ass cheeks. Wasting no time King placed Unique atop the granite countertop. Instead of removing her panties he utilized two fingers pulling them to the side as her wet pussy seemingly jumped into his mouth. Nothing in the kitchen was more fulfilling and tasty than Unique's body. His tongue operated like a rudder on the back of a cruise boat; constantly twirling and kicking up water.

"Daddi this pussy is yours," Unique purred in a state of bliss.

"Tell me again and I'mma make you cum," King remarked in between licking and smacking on her juices.

"Ooh King! Daddi this pussy is all yours!" He focused on her clitoris using the tip of his warm tongue to force her into climaxing frenzy. Unique was in such a state of ecstasy that she placed her hands behind King's head praying that he never took his mouth off her juice box. King's meticulous method of pleasuring Unique with his tongue made her feel as if she had the best pussy in the world. As he raised Unique up carrying her into the room her orgasmic juices moistened his shirt. The taste of her own pussy on his lips was flavorful. King stripped down naked as Unique followed suit. King entered her with his erect penis while simultaneously sucking gently on her succulent breasts. King focused on her total body massaging her thighs, calves, and back never breaching the smooth rhythmic slow stroke pace deep inside her wet pussy walls.

"King I wanna have your baby," Unique moaned meaning every word spoken. King never responded verbally, he simply obliged to her every desire cumming long and hard inside her. Unique wrapped her arms and legs tightly around his naked body refusing to allow his seed out of her garden of Eden.

"King I love you baby and I'll never leave your side," Unique whispered trailing her index nail along his chest.

"I love you too and I know you'll be great mother."

"And you'll be a great father. Let's just keep our fingers crossed."

"Don't worry it'll happen," he assured quelling her worries as they dozed off in each other's arms while King still had his dick wedged within her pussy.

Chapter 17

All I care about is money and the city that I'm from, I'mma sip until I feel it, I'mma sip until it's done... I'm on one, Yeah I'm on one.... Casanova was jamming his pioneer sound system loud as he jumped out leaving the keys in the ignition. He pulled into a decent spot at the car wash prompting NEWPORT SHAWTY to do what he did best; wash cars with a glossed perfection. Casanova was feeling good as his pockets were on swole after a long day of grinding at the Oakland Park Flea Market.

"What dey do bruh-bruh?"

"You already know bout NEWPORT SHAWTY, I stay on the grind," he replied shaking soap suds from his hands in order to remove the cigarette from his lips. Casanova gave him a fist pound then went and took a seat in one of the many plastic lawn chairs. Traffic was rapidly increasing in the area as many people were attempting to claim a spot at the SWAP SHOP drive-in movie theater. Unable to hear his phone ringing Casanova felt it vibrating as it hung on a mesh necklace around his neck.

"What's up wit you cutie?" he asked answering the call.

"Juss leaving the salon. You sound like you at a block party," Deja remarked on the opposite end.

"Naw I'm up here at the car wash."

"Oh okay that's wassup. Well I was wondering if you were gonna be busy tonight?"

"Naw. Why what you up to?"

"I was going out to the Hard Rock and I wanted to know if you would like to keep me some company."

"Yeah I'll roll wit you."

"Alright well make sure you call me when you get home. I'll come get you."

"You know where I stay at?"

"King I haven't forgot where ya mama stay at."

"Nawl I got my own crib in Inverrary now," he corrected her.

"Oh my bad. Well that's even better, I'll come get you from there when you're ready."

"Aiight I'll see you in a lil bit sexy."

"Make sho you call me because I really want to spend some time with you," Deja remarked for assurance as she finally pulled into her Tamarac neighborhood.

"I wouldn't miss being with you for the world bae," Casanova concluded. The candy purple paint job seemed to have an extra sparkle upon it when NEWPORT SHAWTY was finished wiping and waxing to perfection.

"Man what got in dem bottles cause you did ya thang?"

Casanova remarked complimenting NEWPORT SHAWTY's work. Each compliment boosted NEWPORT SHAWTY's ego which Casanova understood as a black entrepreneur the grind could get hard but positive feedback ignites the drive to continue hustling towards prosperity.

"If I told you my secrets then you'd get your own car wash and put me out of business," he replied laughing while tapping an unopened box of Newport cigarettes in his palm.

"You dead right. Same time next week," Casanova commented while dapping him with a fist pound.

"Aiight you be easy out here King," NEWPORT SHAWTY spoke while lighting a fresh cigarette.

"Dats wassup playa."

Two hours later Deja was outside awaiting King's departure from the interior of the townhome. Deja was infatuated with his sense of style and swagger as he stepped out locking the door behind him. King seemed surreal to Deja as he slowly trotted down the five steps in front of the townhome. His body was draped in a thick white cotton Coogi short set as the shorts hung below the knees. The emblem was stitched across the front of the shirt in grey material that seemed to glow in the darkened nightlife. He wore a white & grey pair of retro Air Jordan sneakers that were the exact replica that Michael Jordan wore in the 1997 NBA Finals. A gold ring was wrapped around both pinky fingers while a gold Cuban link hung down below his torso with a customized King of Spades medallion. King walked over to the driver side door of Deja's SUV signifying he'd drive. He helped Deja step out the vehicle whom was dressed to impress as usual. King held her hand as the white leather Sergio Rossi platform red bottom pumps touched the asphalt. White seemed to be her theme for the evening as she wore some BCBG jeans that caressed and loved her curves to perfection. A white form fitting BCBG shirt covered her breasts as the words:

A KING'S QUEEN, was across the front in white embroidery barely visible if not for the diamond studs outlining. A diamond necklace hung atop her chest as matching diamond bangles filled her wrists complemented by similar bangles in her ears.

"You smell good handsome," Deja remarked kissing his lips lightly.

"And the night belongs to you beautiful," he replied leading her around to the passenger door exuding chivalry at it's finest. As King was adjusting the driver seat Deja was strolling through her IPad playlist landing on a song fitting the vibe even through it was throwback; Aaliyah's One In Million. They arrived at the Hard Rock Casino approximately twenty-five minutes later in which the parking lot was filled with vehicles.

"Let's take a few pictures before we go inside," Deja remarked.

Social media here we come, Casanova thought knowing eventually that details of the secret rendezvous would reach Unique's ears and eyes. They posed alternating turns as Casanova eventually stopped a Caucasian couple asking, "Do y'all mind taking a few pictures if us?"

The couple snapped a total of eight pictures of Deja and King hugging and kissing intimately.

"Thank you," King remarked politely showing gratitude retrieving his phone. When they entered the establishment King loaded two Casino gambling cards with one-thousand dollars each informing Deja,

"Babygirl keep your money I got it," handing her a burgundy & black plastic card. For the next three hours gambling and sipping liquor became the focus of the two. GOOD VIBES ONLY! Before it was all said and done Deja profited seven hundred dollars as King doubled up on two-thousand back end profits.

"I think you my good luck charm."

"I was about to tell you the same thang," Deja responded laughing as they were cashing out. Deja was over the edge of just being tipsy so King did all the maneuvering through traffic. Noticing the gloss in Deja's pupils he refused to let her drive home so he parked the pink Mercedes-Benz directly in front of his closed garage.

"Come on in and relax because you ain't driving home til tomorrow," King instructed.

Damn bae I love how you take control, Deja ruminated as King helped her out the vehicle. Deja entered his domain and was immediately impressed with his comfy abode.

"I'mma take a shower and put on one of your tee shirts."

"Dats straight. The shower upstairs in the bedroom." Deja removed her shoes and went upstairs attempting to allow the warm water to sober her mental.

Ooh shit bae got a sexy ass body, Deja thought somewhat shocked as King entered the stand-up shower to join her. They exited the shower together drying each other off with large towels. Deciding to continue the royal treatment King instructed Deja to lay on her belly. King was mesmerized by Deja's tattoo that caused her remind him of one of those Japanese geishas. The mural was one of a kind as the name KING was inked within. King meticulously began applying baby oil on her smooth skin. He made sure that he didn't miss a spot while managing to massage her tense muscles in the process. Deja was completely relaxed under his touch. The more King worked her body with the oil she became extremely horny especially as his smooth touch glided across her ass and inner thighs. She rolled over no longer able to take the blissful teasing stating, "Baby make love to me." Pausing momentarily King adjusted his IPad to a playlist as the first song permeating through the speakers was *Falsetto by The- Dream.* As King penetrated Deja's pussy she moaned with an overdue anticipation, "Aaiigh!"

King stroked her pussy deep and slow as she had tears welling in her eyes. First because the sex felt just that great but most importantly her emotions were overwhelming.

...It's all over now you can come back down...woo sa.., the sultry R&B song continued to play as King paced his hip movements with the rhythm as Deja met each thrust in sync.

"King I wanna have your baby," Deja purred.

King definitely planned to give her what she wanted shifting the pace of his long strokes as the song on the playlist changed with a woman's voice harmonizing over the sounds.

I'm callin you daddi, callin you daddi..., Now I done had it good but it can be better, I done been wet but it can get wetter... Come on daddi rain down on me.... King had Deja on her side digging deep inside her pussy expressing his love with each stroke of his sexual pen. Without warning King ejaculated his essence within Deja's pussy as she moaned.

"Yes daddi give it to me," she purred while tightening her pussy muscles around his dick trapping all the seven within her. King only desired to be delicate with Deja as he spooned cuddling her tight yet gentle. He wasn't confused at all but he knew that he was in love with more than one woman. It was a dilemma that he wasn't sure how to handle but for the time being King would just ride the wave while the tide was high.

"King you my everything. I love you and I'll never disrespect you again."

"It's all good bae," he responded whispering in her ears.

"I hope to have your baby."

"You will bae juss be patient." They were resting momentarily but extra rounds of sex was inevitable. The next round would definitely be a bit kinkier as Deja's sexual libido often switched to over-drive when she had a point to prove.

Chapter 18

Casanova was preparing to leave his place of residence around eleven o'clock a.m. which was a bit later than his usual departing schedule; especially on a working day. *Damn I'm tired,* Casanova ruminated feeling fatigued despite getting adequate rest. The buzzing of his cellphone alerted him of an incoming text message that read:,

Baby I'm pregnant. God is good & life is great! Yayyh to team US.., with Unique's name in the senders inbox. The sudden news caused Casanova instantly sit down even though he was eventually expecting to hear the news. After regaining his composure Casanova texted her back typing:,

Congratulations to the soon to be new Mommy! Make sure you take it easy so we'll bring a healthy baby into this world. Love Always King.... Upon getting dressed Casanova stepped out into the blazing heat elated that in the upcoming months he'd be a father. Soon as he sat in the Cadillac Escalade Casanova had the feeling of deja´vu or more so Deja-vu. His phone buzzed yet again with an incoming text message that shown:, *Hey handsome. I wanted to let you know that soon we're going to be proud parents. Thank you so much. Love your boo Deja....*

King whispered to himself, "I got to be the luckiest yet craziest man alive to get both these women pregnant," as he was texting back simultaneously.

Congratulations to a beautiful soon to be Mommy! I've never been more excited as I can't wait to witness you bring our healthy heaven sent baby into this world. Make sure you take it easy and eat right. Love Always King!... King scrolled through the iPad landing on a throwback hit from Jodeci *Forever my Lady.* He ventured around Broward County clearing his mind deciding that he wouldn't open the shops until near two-thirty p.m. which was when nearby high schools dismissed students with discretionary income. It was Friday and Casanova was certain that people would be straggling in to purchase those last minute weekend outfits. When he finally arrived at the Flea Market there were throngs of teenagers fighting in the parking lot possibly over teenage gossip that amounted to nothing in the real world. King shook his head in a frustrated manner knowing that police would be swarming the scene in a matter of seconds as sirens could be heard blaring in the distance.

I pray my kids don't ever have to go through the foolish teenage wars, he reflected stepping into the ambiance of the daily grind within the Oakland Park Flea Market. A kid in his late teens with a fresh mohawk fade with a design etched within approached King stating, "Man I'm glad you here cause I need a fresh fit fa tonite. Club 54 gon be thick," referring to a happening nightclub in Broward County.

Jit got a lil swag, Casanova ruminated.

"Come on I'mma give you a discount just for waiting."

"Bet dat up!" King peered over his shoulder recognizing qualities he was equipped with propositioning, "If you could work for me on weekends would you do it?"

"In a heartbeat."

"Alright well have ya peeps call me so I can talk to them and we'll go from there," King concluded removing the blue plastic covering his shop's merchandise. "Say less," he replied jubilantly.

The entire morning Meka had been experiencing a pregnancy symptom known as *morning sickness.* Meka knew she was pregnant but had not yet informed King. She would soon tell him but her temporary focus was a mission that a FLAVORED DESIRES employee had set up. If plans were completed she would surprise King with the news. In the meantime Meka refused to have her vision obscured by irrational judgements due to the zygote growing in her belly. She had roughly an hour to arrive at a pre-disclosed location in Palm Beach County. Meka hopped on her Yamaha motorcycle whipping through northbound traffic on Florida's Turnpike. She had been sipping ginger ale so that temporarily curved the light sickness she experienced. Meka's hired female escort alerted her that the particular client was loaded with cash on hand as he was the sole owner of a luxury yacht company. His particular profession had been very lucrative. Despite him regularly requesting the service of FLAVORED DESIRES he was a creep fascinated with filming teenage girls. Meka concocted a plan to use the incriminating information to extort him out innumerable amounts of U.S. currency. Only if the devisive plan worked to perfection. Meka pulled her Yamaha into a self-storage hopping into a Ford Taurus that was parked within. Inside the vehicle was her phony disguise that would allow easy access into the home. The operation was occurring in broad daylight which made the scheme all the more inconspicuous. Meka rang the doorbell dressed in spy-shop gear with phony F.B.I. garments on her person. Unweilding to the guys request Maxine bounced to the door in panties and bra pretending to be the ditzy girl that she wasn't. Meka stepped right in closing the door simultaneously flipping out a phony F.B.I. badge.

"Is Michael Sporato in?" Meka inquired speaking like a seasoned vet. As soon as the words were spoken a short man resembling Danny Devito in every aspect rounded the corner in tropical colored swim trunks with a bulging erection possibly from Maxine's sexual expertise.

"Yes mamm but may I ask why you, an F.B.I. agent is here?"

Okay this lame fuck has bought the gimmick, Meka thought.

"Well the Bureau has been alerted that you've been orchestrating a child pornography business. Do you mind if I search the premises or should I call in a team for assistance?"

"I own a legitimate business and I don't appreciate this despicable accusation."

This perverted piece of shit!, Meka reflected.

"Fine we'll do it the hard way," Meka remarked reaching for her cellphone exposing a gun tucked on the holster on her waist.

"Hold on, hold on let's be reasonable," he responded holding up his palms.

"How much money will it take for you to go away and make a clean report?" he bribed.

Now we talking you sick fucker!, Meka angrily ruminated. "Are you trying to bribe me Mr. Sporato? a Federal Agent."

"Yes. I mean no but yes," he stuttered suddenly feeling the pressure.

"If you have two million in cash right now I'll leave and you and your spouse can continue on. If not then you better pray I don't find anything which I'm sure I will," Meka scowled as if she had years of practice in performing arts school. He was relieved to make the deal as money was nothing to him but his freedom and reputation was everything. As well to continue to record and sell teenage porn on the black market had him creepily elated.

"We have a deal," the short man agreed as Meka towered over him in height. Within five minutes Mr. Sporato stuffed two duffel bags full of cash with a little extra chump change for good measures in hopes God continued to grant him his freedom. Meka put the duffel bags in the car quickly departing knowing that Maxine would slither out of there shortly behind her as was pre-planned.

Damn I shoulda shot his nasty ass in the nuts, Meka thought pulling out the pre-paid cellphone dialing 911.

"Yes I've just witnessed a man in his mid-fifties filming teenage girls naked in his home. Hurry the address is….." Meka informed the operator speaking in a Caucasian's tone with fake tears in hopes to make the police respond to the urgent call speedily. She ended the call then instantly ridded the phone travelling down the turnpike. Meka parked the Ford Taurus back inside the U-Store It shed leaving one of the duffel bags in the trunk which was Maxine's payment. Meka made a smooth getaway on her Yamaha one-million dollars richer. She was anxious to inform King of her newfound wealth but most importantly her pregnancy.

Chapter 19

"Can I come in?" Mr. Dunn asked.

"Yeah close the door behind you," Lacy replied sitting behind her desk.

"I was checking to see if you needed anything. By the way our superiors love the way you handled the client closing that huge deal in the process."

"Send them my gratitude. In the meantime I do need you to please your master," Lacy stated unable to restrain her sexual urges.

"Right here, right now?" he asked somewhat shocked.

"Yes! Now get your ass over here," Lacy exclaimed in a forceful yet seductive tone. Christopher Dunn walked over to Lacy as she spun around in the black leather swivel chair resting her high heel pumps on his shoulders. He placed his head underneath her skirt ripping a hole in the crotch of her stockings licking her pussy like a thirsty puppy while she overlooked the downtown Fort Lauderdale ambiance. Upon constant coaching Christopher had become somewhat better at eating pussy despite nowhere near pleasuring Lacy to the point of ecstasy she craved. Lacy had her hands behind his head fucking his face in an angry manner. Unable to get off Lacy stood placing her palms on the desk whispering,

"Fuck me hard and don't stop til I say so!"

Christopher allowed his polyester slacks to fall to his ankles as he entered her doggystyle with his six-inch penis attempting to do wonders. Lacy moaned in muffled tones more out of frustration than ecstasy vowing to find a way to make King pay for all the mediocre sexual encounters she'd been experiencing due to his negligence of her needs. Lacy's concept was, *How can a man take me on a sexual journey to the highest pinnacles and leave me stranded begging for more without a way of coming down.* Due to the many sex deprived nights, Lacy and Monica both adopted the desire for complete control when it now came to sexual relations with a man. Christopher Dunn with no resistance had become their first mental and physical sex slave.

Chapter 20

"I can't believe these weirdos out here foolin around with our children like that," an older woman resting under the hair-dryer stated while reading the daily Sun-Sentinel newspaper.

"Yeah I know! These people out here sick. I bet they let him out on probation cause he look like he got a bit of money," another customer remarked joining the conversation. Deja listened intently while the women discussed the terror they felt each time their children left the house. Deja devoured an entire bag of grapes occasionally rubbing her growing belly. Unique had gone home early because the last of her appointments were done at four o'clock. Deja employed two other beauticians besides Unique so the bulk of the appointments were easily shared if needed. With an increasing appetite Deja informed her associates that she'd be back shortly. Deja hobbled into her suv trekking down the road to a nearby Taco Bell drive-thru.

"Yes can I have a nacho grande, two soft tacos and one of those Doritos tacos with mild sauce and um that's it," Deja yelled through the intercom.

"That'll be nine o' nine. Drive around to the window," the young teenage employee responded. When Deja circled around to the window there was a familiar face of a pretty teenager whom in her senior year of high school.

"Deja I thought that was you back there. How you doing?"

"Treicy everything is good. Just eating for two now that's all."

"Ooh congratulations! I'll be through the shop next week. Grad nite coming up and I gots to go to Orlando stuntin on dem," Treicy replied smiling.

"Is your twin Neicy coming with you."

"Yes Deja you know how we do."

"Alright don't worry I'mma get y'all right," Deja assured handing her the money. Within minutes Treicy was handing Deja the bag of food that had a savory aroma.

"Alright Treicy you be cool I'll see you later. Tell your sister I said hello."

"I will," she waved. Deja drove down to the CVS Pharmacy on the corner of 441 and Oakland Park Boulevard going inside purchasing a fruit juice because she refused to drink soda. When she made it back to the salon one client remained in which once she departed Deja would close down the salon for the evening.

The aroma of stir-fried chopped chicken breast mixed with brown rice, bell peppers, onions and cilantro leaves covered the kitchen of Unique's apartment. Broccoli with macaroni along with buttered garlic wheat rolls were complementing the dish. Casanova catered the freshly cooked food to Unique whom was sitting in front of the television.

"Thank you bae. When I drop this load I'mma make sure I cook for you."

"Ain't no pressure bae juss relax. My son that you dropping soon is more than enough." Casanova made himself a plate also and relaxed watching television with Unique. Afterwards he rubbed cocoa butter lotion amidst Unique's belly therefore when the birthing process was complete stretch marks would be non-existent.

"So you thought of any names yet?" Casanova asked.

"Major King. How's that sound?" Casanova rubbed his chin contemplating before replying.

"Yeah I like that. Major Ivan King." "Yes bae that's his name because soon as you said that he started kicking. Feel right here he still kicking," Unique informed placing his hand on the right side of her tummy.

"He gonna be very active I can tell cause he ready to come out here into the world," Casanova replied smiling.

"Alright Major calm down you hurting mommy," Unique uttered rubbing her belly in a soothing motion. For the remainder of the night they hung out on the couch as Unique fell asleep on Casanova's lap.

Chapter 21

Days turned into weeks and months as the due dates of Casanova's children was getting nearer by each passing second. The sun had yet to rise as Casanova was wide awake at Meka's place of residence. All night night long he'd been rubbing her belly with cocoa butter lotion while they wrestled joyfully over the perfect name. Understanding that he and Meka both had to be places early caused him to cook a fulfilling breakfast to hold them over until lunch. Turkey sausage, turkey bacon, cheese grits, scrambled eggs, chopped potatoes and lightly toasted bread covered their plates while they tuned into the morning news. They were done eating and out the door by eight as Casanova drove Meka to a luxury car dealership near Fort Lauderdale Airport.

"My sister flight come in at one today so once I pick her up I'll probably be shopping for a while."

"Alright that's cool. You sure you don't need me to wait?"

"Naw I'm good bae. All the paperwork been signed since yesterday. I'm just picking up the keys," Meka assured.

"Okay if you need me you know where I'll be," he

responded kissing her lips lightly. Casanova walked around to the passenger side of the car helping Meka get out the vehicle.

"I, I mean we love you daddi," Meka remarked rubbing her belly hobbling through the double doors.

"I love y'all too." Even though Meka assured him that everything was all right Casanova remained within the dealership's parking lot until he seen Meka driving away in an all-black 760 LI BMW. When he arrived at the Oakland Park flea market Casanova went directly to a jewelry shop where he and a Asian jeweler had become good friends.

"Can you have it ready by tomorrow?" Casanova questioned. The Asian guy nodded his approval as Casanova dropped $8,000 on the glass counter for a down payment.

"You get the rest tomorrow when you finish these pieces," Casanova assured pertaining to the remainder of the cash owed. Everyone knew dealing with the flea market gold precautions had to be taken. Casanova being a connoisseur of fine gold was well aware of the real from the fake. The Asian jewelry guy was customizing three gold diamond bezel medium sized dog tags. The same style that soldiers wore around their necks during war only these were more stylish. Each tag had Casanova's soon-to-be birthed children's names inscribed in cursive within:

Jah Supreme King · Major Ivan King · Nefertiti Euphoria King
   Daddy's Boy   *Daddy's Boy*   *Daddy's Queen*

Deja was giving birth two Jah, Unique would soon be the mother of Major and Meka was birthing a beautiful baby girl in Nefertiti. In the meantime money had to be accumulated so Casanova opened the shop after purchasing two mango salad cups. He took a seat on the barstool in front of the clothing shop reflecting upon the changes within his life. Having a epiphany Casanova utered to himself,

"Yeah I'mma go ahead and sale the other booth. Let me go make my African brother a deal he can't refuse," then began walking towards the fragrance booth.

Over the course of the women's pregnancies Casanova attempted to spread quality time equally amongst them all in which there never seemed to be enough hours in the day. Yet he still maintained, always cherishing the moments he shared with them. He remained true to his promise to Deja as she craved for some seafood cooking. Veering away from fried foods Casanova cooked a healthy yet tasty cuisine. Grilled snapper fish with lemon pepper seasoning as yellow rice mixed with grilled shrimp and chop veggies were an added delight. He also baked fresh butter biscuits that would all be washed down by Tropicana mixed berry blend juice. Deja couldn't have prayed for a better meal. All was well, the sort of calm before the beautiful birthing storm, which a actual Category 3 hurricane was brewing in the Atlantic Ocean.

Chapter 22

Being that a possible hurricane would hit South Florida Casanova advised the ladies to stay at the hospital in case they went into labor before the storm bypassed. Yet in still Casanova had business to handle in which the particular appointment would be his last for a while. The entire time Casanova was venturing out into the streets each of his baby-mommas felt the non-stopping kicks in their bellies as if the unborn children had spiritual premonitions that something wasn't right. Meka informed Casanova about the money she accumulated insisting that he didn't have to work for FLAVORED DESIRES anymore. His persistence to make a final five grand caused her pleading to temporarily subside. Unique and Deja relaxed as much as possible. They were all located in different rooms on the same floor at North Broward General Hospital.

There was an eerie silence on Fort Lauderdale Beach aside from the torrentous rain that poured down rapidly. Crime scene investigators were snapping photos in a meticulous manner careful not to miss any ground breaking clues that would lead to an arrest. The bloody body of Casanova King had just been hauled out the building on life support. What troubled investigators the most was the two laced pantie garments that were intricately placed near his head while he was laying face down fighting for his life.

"Chief we just received a call from the Palm Beach County Police Department. They arrested a man for DUI and guess what, the alcohol mixed with his guilty conscience caused him to tell on himself."

"Let's start the extradition process and get this case solved," Detective Bates responded.

Detective Bates shook his head in disgust as another young black male would possibly lose his life to jealous rage. Whatever the reason for the crime Detective Bates would not rest until the suspect was in his custody and a assured conviction of guilt following. *Damn it looks like he got three children,* Detective Bates ruminated to himself remembering the diamond dog tags around the man's neck as he strolled out the high rise hotel into the pouring rain, wind and lightning illuminating the darkened skies. Onlookers were standing behind the yellow tape shielding their bodies from the cold rain under umbrellas and were petrified as the horrific incident that was not normal in the area was extremely too close for comfort.

Chapter 23

News quickly spread throughout the streets and when the tragic revelation about Casanova King reached the halls of Broward General Hospital there was instant pandemonium. Many women were in delivery screaming loudly as the women whom cared for Casanova were crying and praying at the same time. When a person loved as much as Casanova King is on life support fighting for his life it didn't sit well with anyone. On the morning of September 3, at 6:05a.m. approximately six hours after Casanova was critically shot, Unique gave birth to Major Ivan King whom came out with his eyes wide open destined for greatness it seemed. Nearly one hour later Deja spit out Jah Supreme King whom seemed to refuse to allow his brother to be in world alone without him. Neither of the boys cried during the birthing process which was a possible testament of their father's heart. Meka on the other hand delivered Nefertiti Euphoria King on the same September 3rd but her daughter didn't decide to come out until nine o' clock exactly. To many awakened souls the number mine held a sort of spiritual significance. Ms. Brenda trekked from room to room witnessing the birth of her grandchildren praying her son was spared for blessed opportunity to see his seeds grow. Ms. Brenda rode the elevator a few floors up to I.C.U. to visit her son struggling for his life in a coma. Upon walking to the bedside Ms. Brenda lightly grabbed his cold hands and began to pray.

"Lord God I ask if it be your will please spare my son for his sins. May he be forgiven and given an opportunity to raise his children. Please allow me not to face the heartache of losing my only child. The victory is yours Lord as I rebuke all evil right now tossing it into the lake of fire. We need you Lord.... I pray... Amen," Ms. Brenda concluded nearly five minutes later as tears were streaming down her face.

Upon completion of her supplications Me. Brenda kissed his hand stating, "Alright son it's in God's hands now. All you gotta do is keeping fighting. Fight for your momma," then walked out having faith that God would be God and show up for her. Unbeknownst to Ms. Brenda Casanova had opened his right eye slowly as it was seemly glued shut. *I'll be alright ma just chill,* Casanova thought unable to make a sound as the wooden door swung closed behind his mother departing the room. To Casanova everything seemed to be surreal.

Inside a pale room Christopher Dunn sat nervously chained and shackled awaiting the interrogation process. He hadn't shaved and his eyes were a bright red hue due to the sleepless night filled with guilt and regret. A tall muscular older black gentleman; detective Jeremy Bates to be exact entered the room with his partner; a Latin detective named Raphael Menudo. Everything was being recorded as Detective Bates stated, "Mr. Christopher Dunn are you ready to tell us story of what happened on the night of September 2nd at the Marriott Resort on Fort Lauderdale Beach?" "Yes."

Christopher Dunn paused momentarily then began speaking as his voice resonated in a raspy tone.

"On that particular night I had been downing liquor more than normal because I was so nervous. We, me and two women had rented the suite in my name of course which had become a weekly routine leading up to that night. This was supposed to be another sexcapade as the women liked to call the menage´ a trois´ encounters. They had been ranting about some guy whom they hated which I now know had been avoiding their calls. Sex is all these women wanted and it didn't matter where. When he finally returned their call he was promised twenty-thousand dollars for sexual favors in return which any man in his right mind would accept. When he arrived the women were strutting through the room in panties and bras with those high heels that normally strippers would wear. The women then laid back on the bed as he was explaining that he wouldn't have sex with them and they could keep the money. Before he could turn to leave, I in such a cowardly fashion shot him in the back causing him to fall over face first. I was in such a state of shock that I exited the room not knowing if he was dead or alive."

"What was the reason for the candles throughout?" Detective Menudo asked.

"Well before he arrived me and the ladies had foreplay sex that kept my rational mind induced under their control because I wanted to please them in anyway possible even if it meant killing another man for them."

"We have video surveillance of two women departing through the hotel lobby shortly after the shooting. Do you mind identifying them?" Detective Bates asked pointing to a television screen that was mounted on the wall.

"Yes I'll do it," he concurred pausing momentarily gazing at the screen then remarked, "Yes sir that's them. Lacy Hankerson and Monica Pryce," while shaking his head disgusted with himself.

"Thank you for your cooperation."

"Hold on one more question. What was the deal with the two pair of laced panties placed beside Mr. King's wounded body?" Detective Menudo inquired out of curiosity also wanting all prices of the investigation covered.

"It was supposed to be some kind of symbolical message the women shared with him but I don't know the absolute reason. Well since I cooperated do you think the judge will show leniency?" Christother mentioned gazing back and forth between the detectives seeking some kind of assurance.

"It shows that you have good character and that will definitely be taken into consideration," Detective Bates responded bending the truth knowing full well that State prosecutor would seek maximum penalty.

"Good because I'm hoping to get my job back when this is all over," Christopher remarked exhaling deeply.

This stupid fuck is talking about his job after shooting a man! He'll have a job alright in a fucking prison kitchen, Detective Menudo inwardly thought looking at Christopher with a disgusted stare. As uniformed officers ushered Christopher Dunn outside the interrogation room to be transported back to the Broward County Jail Detective Menudo uttered, "Now we gotta track down the women whom masterminded this entire crime," "To the ends of the earth," Bates agreed lighting a cigarette calmly.

Chapter 24

"Girl this is the life!" Monica stated sipping a pina´ colada flavored martini.

"Yes it is!" Lacy chimed in agreeance.

The two of them were tanning topless poolside in Jamaica enjoying the naked beings prancing around at the Hedonism resort. While they were sitting there chatting two snickers bar complexioned black males approached them wearing no clothing as their penises hung down to mid-thigh.

"Can we have a taste?" the taller of two men asked. Monica and Lacy shared glances exuding the words without speaking , *Hell yeah this is our sexcation!* The men keeled down untying their bikini bottoms and began licking pussy while Monica leaned over sticking her tongue down Lacy's throat. The ladies craved for the long dick's so they raised the men up while turning around on all fours. Monica and Lacy continued to kiss each other while receiving the long hard cock doggystyle. At the particular Jamaican Hedonism resort it was common to witness couples sexually active which possibly stimulated them more knowing that onlookers were watching a live porno.

"Ooh yes fuck me King! Ooh King!" Monica exclaimed unconsciously thinking about Casanova King. The guy thought Monica was calling him a king which aroused him more causing him to stroke rapidly. Lacy looked over realizing that Monica sexed King on that particular office sex encounter even though she constantly denied it. Lacy would occasionally probe which every time Monica would blurt out things igniting suspicions but never had confirmation until the current epiphany.

I'mma whoop yo ass first chance I get you conniving bitch!, Lacy thought as the the large black dick was ramming in and out of her wetness. Even though the sex she was receiving was mind blowing the sound of King's name turned her on more so Lacy started shouting competing with Monica.

"Ooh King! My King! Fuck me!" Monica was so jealous that she participated in the shouting match with Lacy. Breaking the rhythmic pace of the two men was the words spoken by two U.S. Marshall Agents.

"Monica Pryce, Lacy Hankerson! You two are under arrest. You have the right to remain silent…." the agents mentioned as the men slid their bare erect penises from within the women's wet pussies walking away as the women were being handcuffed. The women were screaming many profanities while asking for lawyers which never deterred the U.S. Marshalls from their assigned mission. The Hedonism resort staff provided the agents with white robes to cover the nudity of Monica and Lacy. In the meantime the women were getting a free private flight back to the States to await trial on conspiracy and attempted murder charges. Monica was more upset than ever because she was deprived of a much desired International orgasm experience. *Damn that dick was getting real good too!,* Monica ruminate attempting to remain calm while asking the female agent questions.

"How did you find us?"

The female Marshall never responded as she only stared at Monica venomously with her pupils exuding the words, *Y'all stupid cunts used your passports to flee the country! Not so smart after all you horny nympho bitches!* Within hours the women were back into Broward County law enforcement custody awaiting trial with their male co-defendant.

"Detective Menudo now the fun begins!" Detective Bates remarked upon receiving news about the capture of the accused women.

"I'll make sure I get all the evidence over to the State Attorney's office. I'mma also attempt to get a chance to interrogate the suspects."

"Confirmed. Well in the meantime I'm going to stop by the victim's family residence and inform them about the case at hand," Detective Bates replied.

"Okay partner."

"I'll see you a bit later."

"Take it easy."

"I'll try but for the meantime a strong cup of black coffee is screaming my name," Detective Bates concluded walking out the police station.

Chapter 25

"My son had these dog tags on the night he got shot. I bought three gold rope chains for the kids to wear each one with their name on it," Ms. Brenda stated to all three of King's baby mommas sitting within her living room.

"Did King tell you whether or not he would be there?" Deja questioned anxious to see him.

"It's possible but I don't know. I talked to him a few days ago and he said the physical therapy is over and he's looking and feeling good," Ms. Brenda replied. One by one Ms. Brenda called her grandchildren over whom were one-year olds now, placing the gold chains around their necks. Everyone had mixed feelings and emotions but held it in check because the particular day was an important one.

"Everyone ready to go?" Ms. Brenda asked.

"Yes," all the women replied nearly in unison.

"Alright well the rest of the family will meet us at the courthouse."

On the way to the courthouse Ms. Brenda rode inside the car with Meka and Nefertiti as Deja reconciled her friendship with Unique and rode in the vehicle with the young King boys. The Broward County Courthouse was loaded with people in which the King family entourage nearly filled courtroom 5D to maximum capacity. Many of Casanova's friends and associates were also in the building showing avid support. One of King's uncles wasn't allowed access into the courtroom because during one of Christopher Dunn's pre-trial hearings he interrupted a crucial evidentiary process. King's uncle jumped over the barricade beating the helpless defendant that was cuffed and shackled. To him it was a sort of street vengeance for shooting his nephew. Even if the defendant wasn't cuffed he was too puny to stand a fighting chance against King's angry relative. The State didn't seek to press charges as he was only jailed for a matter of hours then released upon his own recognizance instructed to stay clear of any future trial dates. The particular day was long and eventful especially when Monica Pryce took the stand to offer her testimony.

"Do you swear to tell the truth and the whole truth so help you God?" the judge asked with his right hand raised.

"I do," Monica conceded.

"Proceed with your testimony." Monica rambled on and on as anyone capable of listening could automatically assume she was lying or simply trying to conceal her involvement in the crime. If her lawyer Mr. Richard Perchetti would have known of Monica's incapability on the stand he would have prevented her from speaking. The articulate trickster or in laymen terms state prosecutor struck a nerve with Monica upon asking a question.

"So what was reason for the laced panties? That was quite freaky yet arousing huh?" Instantly Monica spilled the beans as if talking to an erotic novel writer in which her sultry comments would be included.

"Yes the idea was actually one me and Lacy were proud of. On both of our short lived sexual encounters with King he confiscated our panties forcing us to return to our daily working tasks without any. It was quite arousing might I add. We were told each time we thought of the good sexual experience to pleasure ourselves moaning King-ding-a-ling. So to remind him of us we decided to place the panties near his head in hopes he'd never forget about us again," Monica concluded smiling momentarily oblivious that she was on trial for conspiracy and attempted murder.

"I rest my case your honor," the State Attorney remarked having a seat. With the concluding statements of Monica's testimony she literally sealed her and Lacy's fate. She placed them on the scene of the crime as well affirming their masterminded plot. Her statement pertaining to FLAVORED DESIRES, the court counted it as hearsay because Lacy never mentioned it and when investigators searched out the matter the company was non-existent. Meka was sure of this because the company phone was pre-paid and was discarded one year ago along with any information to link and taint King's reputation.

Meka refused to allow that to happen. Some things she'd take to the grave in which King's private business along with the sex tape had been burned. Two days later in that exact same courtroom the jury had reached a verdict. The judge residing began to read off the fate of all three co-defendants.

"Defendant Christopher Dunn the jury finds you guilty of first-degree attempted murder. The State of Florida sentences you to thirty years in custody Department of Corrections custody followed by fifteen years probation." Then he picked up a different folder and continued speaking.

"Lacy Hankerson the jury finds you guilty on charges of conspiracy as well second-degree attempted murder. The State of Florida sentences you to a sixteen year sentence in D.O.C. followed by ten years probation." Upon hearing her fate read off Lacy as well as her mother and father cried. The sudden shift of her life course was totally unexpected in which she still didn't know the exact point where she deviated to cause such a tragic occurrence.

"Monica Pryce the jury also finds you guilty of conspiracy and second-degree attempted murder. The State of Florida sentences you to sixteen years in D.O.C. custody followed by ten years probation. The court is now adjourned." As Monica acknowledged her fate she untied her dreadlocks that were pinned up in a bun. She turned to the cold stares of all three of Casanova's baby mommas silently mouthing, *I'll be back bitches!,* as the bailiffs ushered her out the courtroom to a holding cell. The women were anxious for a brawl inwardly praying to one day get their hands on Lacy and Monica. Upon making it outside Casanova's father gathered the entire family preparing for a brief speech. Before speaking he was momentarily in a trance thinking, *Damn that's a bad ass car. Gotta be somebody important,* noticing a 2014 Rolls Royce Wraith. The pearl white paint job caused the moving vehicle to seem angelic as all heads began to turn and stare because it was rare to see a two-door Rolls Royce. The vehicle came to a halt in front of the King family entourage. As the door opened a size 9 ½ all white Gucci loafer touched the pavement seceded by the other foot. Casanova King stood tall draped in an all white linen short set causing instant joyful pandemonium. Before even speaking a word he gave each of his baby mommas a kiss on the cheek careful not show any favoritism. He hugged his children tightly showering his baby girl with many kisses causing an onpour of smiles and giggles. The love triangle was strange but each one of his baby mommas were grateful to have some of him then no King at all. Upon giving his mother a hug and kiss on the cheek he embraced his father and uncles with a manly hug. Deciding to allow his son to speak Casanova's father stepped aside.

"First and foremost I want to thank everyone for your support. As a family we stuck together and made it through the tough times. God is good as all prayers were heard. New days cause for a celebration and I want to show my gratitude to each and every one of you. I reserved an entire floor at the Westgate Resort in Orlando as well purchased armbands for all for all the Walt Disney theme parks for us to enjoy as a family. I got a lot of making up to do but I know God will lead me. I know I can't keep my car in the middle of the road like this but before we leave Pops I want you to lead us in a quick prayer," Casanova concluded as everyone joined hands. Casanova couldn't have prayed for a better family. In the hearts and panties of many women he served as clients, his memory would forever be stained in their orgasmic roledex. Rumor has it that when life enters the world one leaves in which this case the rumor was proven to be fabricated statistics. Once people are cultivated to do away with the deadly sins of adultery, fornication, uncleaness, wrath, strife, greed, envy, murder and lasciviousness then the world would be perfect but at the same time life would not be exciting. So until the society known to be called the hood becomes perfect ladies be careful with the removal of your laced under garments and fellas many pretty panties come with complicated retributions so be careful of those beautiful conniving nymphos draped in enticing *Laced Panties.....*

Epilogue

Monica Pryce had been an inmate at a women's correctional facility for nearly five years in North Florida. Up until today Monica had been everything a model inmate is supposed to be. For the last two months she had her eyes feasting upon her classification officer. Today she was up for her yearly review in which this go-around she was eligible for a good adjustment transfer as she hoped to re-unite with Lacy at a different facility. For the meantime Monica was preparing to work her "ass"-ets to seduction.

"Monica Pryce," a young, black, descent looking male classification officer called out.

I'm bout to get me some of dat dick, Monica ruminated innocently strutting to the back where his office was located closing the door behind her.

"I see you've had no D.R.'s in the last five years which shows you've been behaving like a reformed inmate seeking a change," he stated gazing at the computer screen before him.

"Yes that's right but I'm desiring to be naughty, will you please spank me," she replied seductively approaching allowing her pants to drop exposing a freshly shaven pussy. Only a non-heterosexual male would have dismissed Monica's advance. He couldn't turn down a pretty pussy as he entered Monica from a standing doggystyle position. Monica grinned sinisterly inwardly shouting, *Yes I got you right where I want you,* as her classification officer was unaware of her desire to have absolute control utilizing sex as a means to accomplish it. Her sexual needs were finally being fulfilled after a failed Hedonism orgasm years prior. From that moment on she'd attempt to have complete sexual control of an ongoing sexcapade between inmate and staff member. Always the lure of the panties….